How To Use Your

Decide Your Destiny Book

Follow the instructions below before reading this book.

1. Go to: www.doctorwhochildrensbooks.co.uk/decideyourdestiny

2. Click 'Begin' to launch the book selection screen.

3. After selecting your book, the scene selection menu will appear.

4. Start reading the story on page 1 of this book and follow the instructions at the end of each section.

5. When you make a decision that takes you online, select the correct box and enter the corresponding code word as prompted.

6. After watching the scene or completing your online activity, return to the scene selection screen and continue your story.

Now turn the page and begin your adventure!

DOCTOR ᴅⱳ WHO

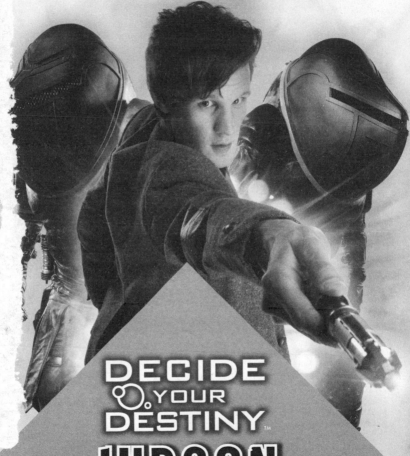

DECIDE YOUR DESTINY

JUDOON

BBC CHILDREN'S BOOKS
Published by the Penguin Group
Penguin Books Ltd, 80 Strand, London, WC2R 0RL, England
Penguin Group (USA) Inc., 375 Hudson Street, New York 10014, USA
Penguin Books (Australia) Ltd, 250 Camberwell Road, Camberwell, Victoria 3124, Australia
(A division of Pearson Australia Group Pty Ltd)
Canada, India, New Zealand, South Africa
Published by BBC Children's Books, 2010
Text and design © Children's Character Books, 2010
Written by Oli Smith
10 9 8 7 6 5 4 3 2 1
BBC logo © BBC 1996. Doctor Who logo © BBC 2009. TARDIS image © BBC 1963.
Licensed by BBC Worldwide Limited.
BBC, DOCTOR WHO (word marks, logos and devices), and TARDIS are trademarks of the
British Broadcasting Corporation and are used under licence.
ISBN: 978-1-40590-697-5
Printed in Great Britain by Clays Ltd, St Ives plc

'Yes, it's space.'

The Doctor's voice breaks your concentration and you finally turn away from the open Police Box doors to look at the trio leaning casually over the railings by the console. The Doctor, Amy and Rory.

'Or, as I like to call it, outer space,' continues the strange man with the bow tie and the eyes that seemed much older than their years.

The Doctor, Amy and Rory in the TARDIS. 'Travelling through time and space,' they'd said, but you'd not believed it until you'd turned to leave the impossibly large control room to return home – and instead found a vast expanse of stars and nebulae stretching out forever beyond those blue wooden doors. You should have realised that the bottom of your garden was a strange place to put a Police Box right from the start.

'Well, you're here now; you may as well make the most of it,' the fiery-haired girl had said in her comforting Scottish accent, with a gentle smile. And you'd nodded and smiled back, relieved by the reassuring wink her husband had given you.

'Can you close the doors, please? It's getting a bit chilly in here.' The Doctor is already at the console, yanking levers, banging panels and generally not being very gentle. 'I think, considering the shock we've given our new guest, we should go somewhere a little more... cosy,' he finishes with a grin.

No sooner have you closed the doors than you are off, hurtling through the Time Vortex with a wheeze and groan of engines! The journey takes either a few seconds or several hundred years – depending on how you look at it – and you're not sure which it is yourself, but with a loud, echoing thud you suddenly realise that you've landed.

Cautiously, you pull open the doors one more time and step outside into a lush, tropical jungle. The deep heat of an alien summer makes you catch your breath as the Doctor fumbles around in his jacket pockets for the key to the TARDIS door, retrieving it with a triumphant 'ah!'

Amy rubs her hands together. 'So, why are we here, Doctor?' she says, eager to solve a new mystery.

The Doctor looks up at the overcast sky. 'Didn't I tell you?' he replies. 'This human colony on the planet Betul is home to one of my favourite tea shops.' He stamps his feet excitedly. 'And I'm in the mood for a cuppa!'

You walk together through the small wooden village, peering through half-open windows, looking for the source of all the wonderful smells and sounds around you. The forest behind falls away to reveal low-hanging vines and you can smell the sea. You can hear the low chatter of the villagers, the odd snatch of song from a fuzzy radio and the regular tapping of hammers as the townsfolk prepare their homes for the summer rains.

Soon you are perched on a very pleasant wicker chair by the banks of the sea, listening to the creak of the floorboards as water laps beneath them. It's not quite the exciting adventure the Doctor had warned you about when you first agreed to come along for a ride, but when Mr and Mrs Azzopardi, the soft and kindly owners of the shop, emerge with a tray and four china cups of tea, you are soon relaxing and chatting like four friends on holiday.

Suddenly the cups on the table start to shake, their clattering joined by a low rumble. You look up into the sky. 'There!' Rory points.

Three dark shapes are lowering themselves ominously through the grey sky, like three giant skyscrapers. They disappear into a bank of storm clouds on the horizon and the Doctor leaps to his feet.

'Oh dear,' he says. 'Oh dear, oh dear, oh dear! And I was having such a lovely afternoon.' He hops over the table legs and starts running towards the tiny harbour you spotted on the way to the café.

'Wait! Where are you going?' Amy calls after him.

'To find out what those pesky Judoon want. Back in a mo!'

Amy looks just as puzzled as you. Judoon? She glances around nervously.

'I don't like the look of those clouds.' Rory nods at the horizon. 'I reckon there's a storm approaching – that's why it's so humid and wet. It could break any minute. Best try and persuade the Doctor not to go out on the water 'til it passes.'

If you decide to take Rory's advice and try to persuade the Doctor to return, go to 3.

If you decide to jump up and join the Time Lord, go to 2.

The Doctor is already picking his way across the low scaffold of wooden planks that span the marshland of the coast by the time you catch up with him. Your shoes slip on the narrow beams but you manage to avoid landing in the brown sludge beneath the walkways.

The Doctor turns at the sound of planks rattling behind him and reaches out a hand to balance you as you jump to join him on a sturdier part of the scaffold.

'So, you decided to come and see the action for yourself, did you?' He smiles and pats you absent-mindedly on the shoulder. 'Good, I like that.'

You walk on for a few seconds towards the harbour. It's only a small cluster of rowing boats tied loosely to poles but you can see that it's the heart of the village: bustling fishermen and women walking hurriedly to and from the boats, transferring the last nets of a weird, pink fish to the storehouses before the inevitable rains.

'So, Amy and Rory didn't want to come?' the Doctor sighs. 'I suppose it's probably for the best – we'd never have all fitted into one boat.'

On the horizon, a haze of white fog is already transforming into rolling storm clouds, and in the distance you can hear the faint crack of thunder.

'The monsoon is building; we'd better get a move on.' The Doctor hurries onto a nearby jetty. 'The atmospheric disturbance from the

Judoon ship's engines won't have helped either.'

He points to the furthest end of the harbour, where the last rowing boat is being moored by a small old man with a woolly hat pulled down over his weathered face. 'It looks like that's the last boat. Hurry, before he covers it over for the storm!'

Go to 4.

You agree with Rory: it would be far too dangerous to risk getting trapped out in the open when the rains hit, let alone out at sea in the fog.

'Doctor!' Rory shouts, getting up and running over to the retreating figure. 'Don't you think it would be better to ask around the village first? Try and discover why these aliens might want to come to Betul?'

After a lot of hand waving and loud talking from Rory, the Doctor reluctantly agrees and returns to the porch of the café. He slumps into his creaky wooden seat with a grumble of 'no fun any more...' and fiddles with his bow tie.

'Right, well before you start complaining about us running off towards certain death, why don't you tell us what exactly these Judoon are?' Amy says as she sips her tea.

The Doctor finishes his cup, clattering it onto the saucer. 'The Judoon are intergalactic policemen,' he explains. 'But not the friendly, offer-to-give-you-directions-and-help-lost-children-find-their-parents-at-the-fair type. They're more the thuggish, break-down-your-door-and-set-fire-to-your-living-room-before-discovering-they-have-the-wrong-house type. I'm sure whoever's in trouble on Betul has good reason to be, but it's the human colonists here I'm worried about – there's nothing worse than getting in the Judoon's way.'

'And what was it you wanted us to do again, Doctor?' Rory asks innocently.

'Get in their way,' the Doctor replies.

Go to 5.

You run over just as the old man is about to drag a tarpaulin over his small wooden rowing boat, its oars tucked safely inside.

'Oh, hello.' He throws you a nervous half-wave. 'I've not seen you around here before. Are you local?'

The Doctor steps in with his customary pumping handshake and cheery 'how do you do? I'm the Doctor' routine. After introducing both you and himself, he continues. 'We're just tourists, you see. Your quaint village tea shop is quite something around these parts of the galaxy, you know.'

The old man seems to soften. 'Well, that's very kind of you to say so, Doctor. My name is Sean and I live a few doors down from the Azzopardis.' His face grows a little sterner. 'But I don't think you two should be out here in weather like this – the monsoon is about to break and we're all heading for shelter.' He leans in further and whispers. 'It's not just the rain that comes in from the sea, you know.'

The Doctor raises his eyebrows. 'You don't say. Well, I love a good monster myth. Plenty of tourist spots have those: Loch Ness and... well, actually that's the only one I can think of right now.' He throws a quick glance in your direction. 'Now Sean, I hope it won't be too much trouble, but if you could just wait right here for a second, I'd like to discuss something with my young friend.'

The Doctor strides over to you, a friendly arm wrapped around your shoulders, and turns you both so that Sean cannot hear his next words. 'You see, I was right,' he whispers urgently, 'there is something fishy going on. We need to get out to sea and find out what, and Sean's is the only boat that's not been tied down for the night. What do you think we should do?'

If you decide to go ask Sean if you can borrow his fishing boat for a while, go to 6.

If you suggest to the Doctor that you 'borrow' it without Sean's permission, go to 7.

There is silence in the café for a few moments as the Doctor shifts impatiently in his chair, waiting for the rest of the group to finish their tea. Through your clothes you can feel the breeze picking up as the storm clouds loom menacingly overhead. You listen to the ominous creak of the building as the wind begins to whistle through the cracks. But then you hear something else: a rustling sound coming from beneath your chair.

Looking down, you find a battered newspaper; someone must have left it there from earlier in the day. You pick it up, folding it so that you can see the front page, which reads:

As the Monsoon Approaches, Will the Ghost Town Strike Again?

Underneath is a grainy black and white photograph: the dark silhouette of a shanty town floating in the sea!

'What's that you've got there?' Amy asks over your shoulder. You hand over the paper and watch as she reads the headline and shivers.

'Wow,' she says. 'Spooky.'

'What is?' Rory asks. He holds out his hand for the paper but the Doctor reaches in between them and snatches it from Amy's grasp with a swift 'yoink!'

The Doctor scans the pages. 'Oh dear,' he says. 'This doesn't look good. This doesn't look good at all. No wonder the Judoon are involved.'

'I didn't finish!' Amy says angrily.

The Doctor clears his throat. 'Are you all sitting comfortably?' He peers over his nose at the group. 'Then I'll begin.' And he starts to read aloud.

If you have access to a computer, click on box A on screen and enter the code words DAILY BETUL.

If you do not, go to 98.

'You're right,' the Doctor grins at you, 'honesty is the best policy.' Together you turn back to Sean, the Doctor scratching his nose as he tries to phrase the question. 'Now Sean, I know we've only just met, but you seem like a nice fellow and I was wondering if you could do us a favour.'

The old man raises an eyebrow. 'Oh yeah?' he says. 'And what might that be?'

The Doctor jumps straight to the point, gesturing to the end of the jetty. 'Your boat – I was wondering if we could borrow it, only for an hour.' He holds up his hands. 'Not long at all, really.'

'But–' Sean begins.

'Yes, yes, I know – the whole monsoon thing,' the Doctor interrupts. 'But I give you my word, we'll only be a moment, and if we don't get it back to you in one piece, I will personally build you a replacement. How does that sound?'

There is a tense pause as the fisherman considers for a second. 'Well, you do seem like nice fellows, and you do like the tea...' The Doctor nods, encouraging the man to continue. Finally he relents. 'Oh, all right, you can take it, but if you go off and get killed in that storm I won't be a happy fisher!'

The Doctor is already untying the boat from the jetty before Sean has even finished. He throws you an oar, laughing. 'You needn't worry about that, Sean – I make a habit of not dying, whatever the odds!'

As you get aboard the wobbling craft, the Doctor gives a final wave and shout of 'goodbye!' to the bewildered fisherman, before pushing off from the bank and out into the open sea.

If you have access to a computer, click on box B on screen and enter the code words JUDOON TOWERS.

If you do not, go to 9.

'Are you sure about that?' The Doctor raises an eyebrow. 'It seems a bit underhand to me. It's your call though.' He turns around. 'Sean?' But the fisherman has disappeared. The Doctor runs a hand through his long fringe. 'I thought I told him to stay right there! Ah well, I guess we should take that as a sign.'

Quickly, you both make your way to the end of the jetty, wincing with every creak of the boards beneath your feet. The Doctor jumps into the small rowing boat whilst you leap into action, untying the craft from its moorings.

'I knew it!' comes a voice from behind you. The Doctor's arms flail as he loses his balance in the boat, throwing him back onto the jetty. It's Sean. He is holding a piece of rope in his hands and his face is red and furious.

'I leave you alone for one second to get an extra bit of rope and you immediately decide to thieve my boat!'

'We can explain!' The Doctor raises his hands to try and calm the situation.

'No, I should never have trusted a bunch of...' he spits the words, 'tourists! Get out of my sight!'

You take the Doctor by the arm and lead him sheepishly back to the café, where Amy and Rory are still finishing their tea.

Go to 5.

You grin, ready for action. Where does the Doctor want to start?

'It's your call. Do we return to the colony and see if we've missed anything that might help? Or head straight to the Varna settlement and offer them a chance to explain themselves?' He looks at his watch. 'We'd better hurry though; the Captain wants to leave any second.'

The Judoon hanger bay is a huge expanse of ribbed metal struts that houses a rank of squat landing craft made of reinforced steel plates. Large landing hatches stand open at the end of each transport and squads of Judoon move to and fro between them, performing last-minute checks before embarkation. You join the Doctor as he steps forward into a pool of bright white light where the Judoon captain and his squad are gathered around a sonar map of the surrounding area.

Barking loudly over the noise of the preparations, the captain gestures at the two lights pinpointed on the map. Situated along the ragged edge of the coastline, the first light clearly indicates Colony Seven, whilst further out to sea the second marker is labelled 'Illegal Varna Settlement'. It shifts gently as the sonar sweeps across the map once more, updating its coordinates.

'As you can see,' the captain continues, 'the Varna settlement is already on the move. We need to act quickly before they attack the colonists.'

He turns his dull brown eyes towards you and the wrinkled skin of his brow furrows as he waits for your decision. 'Choose our destination.'

With one eye on the Doctor, you raise your finger...

If you decide to return to the colony, go to 70.

If you press on to the Varna settlement, go to 71.

You watch the coastline diminish behind you as the Doctor sits in the bow, rowing with gusto. Away from the shore the air is colder and you shiver as the damp fog swallows your craft. Soon the green jungles of the coast are a shadowy blur and even the Doctor seems to be struggling to keep his bearings.

Suddenly the air becomes fresher, the grey fog turning white as sunlight breaks through the mists above your head. The Doctor tucks the oars under his seat as the boat drifts into the strangely still clearing, only the ripple from the bow of the ship breaking the calm of the water.

'We must be near the landing site; atmospheric disturbance caused by their engines would have punched a hole in the rain clouds.'

You're just relieved to see the sky, bathing your face in the pink light of an alien star.

'Stop sightseeing, we've arrived.' The Doctor points over your shoulder. 'The Judoon ships.'

You turn to look, straining your eyes to see the summits of the huge metal pillars covered in bolted panels and rivets, a trio of skyscrapers, half-submerged in the ocean, but still towering over your little boat.

'You should see the look on your face,' the Doctor grins. 'So, what do you think? Shall we hail them, or try and slip in under the radar?'

If you want to hail the Judoon ship, go to 60.

If you decide to try and sneak on board with the Doctor, go to 61.

'Scary stuff,' says Rory.

The Doctor nods silently, deep in thought.

'Well, whatever it is that's attacking them, I don't think we'll have too long to wait.' Amy is holding her hand outside of the wooden canopy protecting the porch. Large drops of water are falling on her hand, and suddenly the clouds break!

Huge sheets of water crash down on the café with a roar, the sea barely visible through the downpour.

The Doctor leaps from his chair, pulling his jacket over his head to ward off the rain. 'What shall we do?' he yells over the noise.

Amy turns to you. 'I think we should get inside the café and bolt the doors. I'm sure the owners won't mind – anything could happen out here and we won't be able to solve this mystery if we drown!'

'We can't do that!' Rory shouts. 'If we take shelter we might miss finding out what the ghost town actually is. Come on, I want to see the action first hand. Water never did anybody any harm!'

'Well, that's not strictly true...' the Doctor interrupts, but is silenced by a hard stare from Amy. He turns to you. 'Well, it looks like you've got the casting vote,' he says. 'What's it going to be? Shelter or adventure?'

If you want to leave your investigation until after the storm blows over, go to 11.

If you agree with Rory and decide to stay outside, go to 12.

You don't waste a second. Yanking open the door to the interior of the café, you burst in, closely followed by Amy, the Doctor and, reluctantly, Rory. The bell above the shop door tinkles for a moment in the soft silence of the café until suddenly you realise that you can hear a whimpering coming from behind the rough wooden counter.

Amy is there before you can blink. 'Mr and Mrs Azzopardi!' she calls over, as she reaches down to lift the terrified woman to her feet with a little help from her husband.

'We thought you were those creatures from the ghost town!' Mrs Azzopardi sniffs through her tears.

Amy wraps an arm around her shoulders. 'Oh, don't worry about them, we're here now, we'll look after you both.'

'Yes, safety in numbers.' Mr Azzopardi states gruffly as he straightens his dusty tie.

The Doctor asks you to help out making another round of tea, but Rory still seems to be in a huff. 'There might be safety in numbers in here, but if we were outside we could be getting to know our enemy — isn't that more useful?'

'Sometimes, Rory, the human approach is the one that leads to the happiest solutions.' The Doctor frowns. 'Right now, these poor scared people need our help and I'm glad our friend here persuaded us to take shelter.' He looks at you and smiles.

Go to 13.

'You're right: we have to face our fears.' The Doctor nods and looks at his watch. 'Keep your eyes peeled, everybody, it can't be long now.'

Keenly you scan the murky haze of the storm as it sinks low over the seafront and over the town, the water a mess of ripples and splashes until, suddenly, you spot it: over to the left, a dark shape approaching through the rain.

You warn the others and they turn to look. In front of you, Amy grabs Rory's hand nervously as the shape approaches and becomes more definite. You can see the jumbled angles and points of rooftops, chimneys, windows and wooden staircases. A shiver runs down your spine. It really is a floating town, a wide deck supported by what looks like hundreds of wooden barrel supports. Tattered black sails billow in the breeze as it shudders closer and closer.

'It doesn't look like much of a ghost town to me,' the Doctor says, unimpressed. 'More like a real town made of wood.'

'That doesn't mean the population couldn't be ghostly,' Rory replies.

'Okay, two things there,' says the Doctor, holding up a finger. 'Firstly, what would ghosts want with a real town? Secondly, and this is the important one, ghosts don't exist.'

As the town approaches the shore a sudden chill spreads through your bones and you can feel the hairs on the back of your neck begin to prick up. You hope that the Doctor is right; he's never been wrong before, has he?

Go to 14.

'Quiet!' The Doctor interrupts the chatter of introductions and hand shaking. 'Listen!' Everyone stops, ears pricked up.

Over the roar of the rain another noise begins to emerge, a low chattering and shrieking, the sound of footsteps on walkways, growing in intensity. You hold your breath as the noise draws closer before, suddenly, Bang! Bang! Bang!

You jump as something hammers on the locked door of the café.

Bang! Bang! The door shakes, its hinges rattling under the strain, but the wooden bolt holds fast. Nobody breathes.

'What do we do?' Mrs Azzopardi squeaks.

The Doctor looks to Rory. 'Well, you wanted to meet your enemy. Why don't you answer it?'

Rory looks at his shoes. 'You know what? I'm okay at the moment, actually. Maybe we should just wait for whoever it is to calm down before saying hi.'

The Doctor rolls his eyes.

Do you keep quiet and hope that the creature goes away? Go to 15.

Or do you face your fears and open the door? Go to 19.

With a huge thud and a great amount of creaking the town hits the shore, only a few houses down from the café porch. Even from that distance you can see dark shapes moving across the jumble of buildings, inhuman silhouettes jumping from staircase to staircase. Over the breezy chatter of the rain you hear the rising warble of alien voices as the shapes spill out into the village, their legs clacking on the walkways as they leap from building to building, hammering on the doors.

Human screams fill the air and you spin around at the sound of a wooden bolt being flung back in the café behind you. An old couple burst out onto the porch and stop short at the sight of you.

'Mr and Mrs Azzopardi!' the Doctor shouts, 'Don't you think it would be safer to stay indoors?'

'You must be out of your mind!' the old woman replies. 'I can hear the screams from inside; we're getting away from here as fast as we can.' You can see that she is trembling with fear, clutching her husband's arm for support. '*The Daily Betul* can stuff its nonsense about staying resolute in the face of death!'

And with that they are gone, running and dodging between the buildings, heading inland towards the rainforest.

'Um, Doctor?' Amy calls, 'I think those things might be coming this way!'

'Quick, hide!' Rory yells, dragging you towards a pile of barrels by the waterfront beside the porch. 'And get ready to make a break for the TARDIS!'

Go to 16.

Bang! Bang! Bang!

The door shudders once more. 'Keep. Quiet.' The Doctor holds a finger to his lips. 'Not a sound.'

The room falls into darkness as Mr Azzopardi extinguishes the lamps and you huddle in the corner of the café for what seems like an eternity.

Suddenly, there is a violent shaking as something tries the handle of the door, rattling the lock in its socket. Mrs Azzopardi jumps and covers her mouth to stifle a scream.

There is a pause. Then, slowly, the sound of footsteps on the porch outside can be heard retreating into the distance. You heave a sigh of relief as the danger retreats – for now.

'Listen.' Amy points to the roof. 'The rain is easing off.'

Cautiously, Mr Azzopardi reaches for the nearest lamp and flicks the switch. In the sudden pool of light you can see the Doctor looking around, a sly grin spreading across his face in sharp contrast to the frightened expressions of the rest of the group.

'Right,' he says, rubbing his palms together. 'Who's for taking a look outside?'

Go to 17.

You duck behind the barrels just in time as a group of the creatures lope onto the porch of the café. Their hideous forms are a dripping combination of beetle-shell and gooey flesh, their mouths bristle with pincers and each of their four limbs sports a cross between a horse's hoof and a nasty-looking claw. You give Amy a look as she sharply draws breath, but she remains silent.

The creatures' feet click against the wooden decking of the porch as they approach the open door to the café, slamming it open with a spindly arm, and ducking as they enter the darkened interior.

The Doctor winces as crashing sounds emerge from the café, tea cups flying out onto the porch and shattering on the wet wood. 'That was my favourite tea shop,' he says, crestfallen.

Then he stands up cautiously, looking around.

'What are you doing?' Amy hisses.

'Oh, hush. They're distracted at the moment. I think it's time to have a look at what's actually going on,' he replies.

Reluctantly you get up and follow the Doctor around the side of the café until you can see down one of the side streets. Chaos has taken over and in the distance you can see the dark shapes of the creatures flitting from building to building.

'See? No bodies – they aren't attacking the humans, just trashing their homes.' The Doctor rubs his chin, deep in thought. 'But why would a ghost town want to invade a colony simply to muck around with the furniture?'

Go to 18.

The town is eerily silent. Your footsteps and the steady hiss of the rain are the only sounds in the empty streets. Amy looks cautiously down one of the alleyways, her face falling at the destruction she can see: torn sheets, broken chairs and still-warm food lying strewn across the wood decking. 'I think we might be the ones in the ghost town now,' she whispers.

'Hopefully the townsfolk have fled into the safety of the jungle,' the Doctor replies.

'Either that, or they've been taken prisoner,' Amy retorts.

The Doctor cocks his head to one side, considering. 'They'd need a pretty big ghost town to do that,' he says, before giving a harsh laugh. 'You know, I can't wait to find out what we're actually dealing with so that I can stop calling it a 'ghost town'!' He waggles quotation marks in the air with his fingers.

By now you're walking up to a crossroads between the houses and in the gap between the buildings on your right you can make out a familiar dark shape by the seafront. But there's something strange about the jumbled outline of the ghost town – it seems to be shrinking…

You call the group to a halt, pointing in the direction of the floating shadow. The Doctor screws up his face as he tries to make out what's happening through the mist. Looking closer, you can see dark shapes spilling out onto the floating shape; the creatures are returning home.

You make your way carefully to the edge of the colony, just in time to see the ghostly town disembark from the shoreline and begin floating silently out to sea.

'They're leaving!' Amy whispers.

'Well,' says Rory with a sigh, 'I guess that means we're on clean-up duty!'

But his words are cut short by a shrill cry from somewhere in the town, an unearthly scream that forces Amy to cover her ears. 'What's that?' she yells over the noise.

If you decide to investigate the noise, go to 25.

If you are worried that it could be a trap and want to wait and see what happens, go to 26.

Rory shuffles around behind you until he is next to the Doctor, nervously looking about him as he whispers urgently in the Time Lord's ear. 'Don't you think we should take this opportunity to get back to the TARDIS whilst we're still unnoticed?' he says.

The Doctor raises his eyebrows. 'Really? I was going to suggest taking the opportunity to sneak on board that ghost town of theirs. That seems like much more fun!'

Rory's shoulders visibly droop.

Amy walks over to him and gives him a hefty pat on the back. 'Hey, it was your idea to confront the creatures!' she says with an affectionate smile.

You point out that if you're going to try and sneak on board, you're running out of time. The Doctor agrees. But Amy suddenly stops and Rory turns in surprise.

'Aren't you coming?' he asks.

She considers for a moment. 'No. Someone has to make sure the villagers are all right. Who knows what may have happened to them? They might need our help, especially the Azzopardis. We can't just run off and leave them!'

The Doctor seems pleased. 'That's my Amy!' he says. 'Fine, we'll stick around and make sure the colonists are okay.'

You stand there for a second, suddenly confused. This could be your only opportunity to get onto the ghost town and find out what the creatures want!

If you suggest that Amy and Rory stay behind whilst you and the Doctor investigate the ghost town, go to 20.

If you decide that you all should stay and make sure everyone is all right, go to 17.

If no one else will do it, you will! You leap over to the front door and slam the bolt back before anyone can stop you. But the door crashes inward, sending you flying back against the wall as one of the creatures bursts into the room! A hideous sight, its mouth is filled with pincers, and its gooey flesh is covered in what looks like large black beetle shells. It raises its arms dramatically to reveal hoof-like claws and lets out an unearthly scream, matched in intensity only by Mrs Azzopardi as she howls in terror!

The room freezes for a second as the monster looms over them, then it roars again!

'All right, all right, we get it!' the Doctor yells over the noise.

The creature stops roaring. It looks slightly confused. Then it lowers its head and thrusts its face at the Doctor. You wince, waiting for the monster to attack when suddenly, from the corner of your eye you see Amy, gesturing furiously at something behind you.

You look around and see a large china teapot on the floor under one of the tables. Amy mouths something at you.

'Use it on the alien!'

You pick up the teapot; it feels solid and heavy in your hand. Should you use it? There are only a few seconds left to decide as the creature's pincers descend towards the Doctor's head!

If you decide to smash the teapot over the monster's head before it can attack the Doctor, go to 21.

If you cannot bring yourself to use the weapon, go to 24.

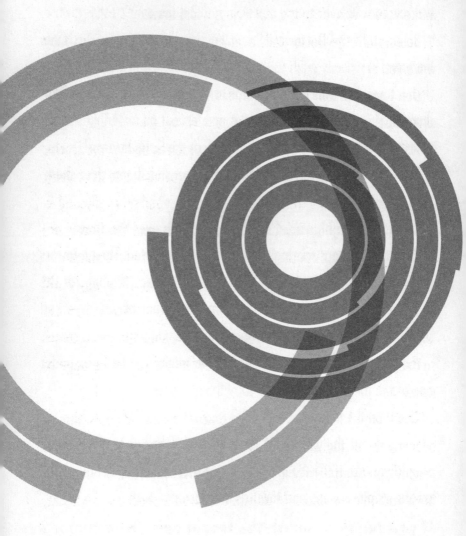

With a brief goodbye to Rory and Amy, you and the Doctor begin to make your way over to the mysterious ghost town.

'Be careful!' the Doctor calls over his shoulder to the pair as they wave you off.

'Don't worry about us!' Amy smiles. 'We know how to look after ourselves.'

'Well, you know how to look after yourselves badly,' the Doctor replies – but the couple have already wandered back into the colony.

You pick your way carefully over the bank, your shoes slipping in the mud beneath your feet, and soon both you and the Doctor are wading knee-deep through the water towards the floating village.

'We'll circle around the side,' the Doctor whispers. 'That way it will be easier to avoid detection.'

Your clothes feel heavy in the cold water and soon the sea becomes so deep that you have to swim the final few metres to the edge of the deck.

'This is why I like being tall,' the Doctor says as he hauls himself over the top of the wooden planks with ease, wincing as the barrels beneath creak and roll in the water. He reaches out a hand and helps you onto the deck. 'Quickly, move into the shadows,' he hisses, dragging you out of sight.

You flatten yourself against the wall of one of the weirdly deformed houses that are packed onto the large timber base and begin wringing out your clothes whilst the Doctor keeps a lookout.

Go to 80.

The teapot shatters with a satisfying crash over the monster's solid head, sending its body thundering to the floor in a pile of limbs and claws. You stand there, stunned, the teapot handle hanging from your fingertips.

'Blimey.'

The Doctor swallows, straightening his bow tie and grimacing as his fingers encounter the sticky layer of goo on his shirt that the creature had drooled.

'I'm not trying to sound ungrateful here, but was that absolutely necessary?' asks the Doctor.

'Of course it was necessary, that thing was about to bite your head off, Doctor!' Rory gets slowly to his feet, brushing sawdust from his jeans. 'Now we need to decide what to do with him.'

Amy is already at the open door, peering keenly into the grey mist outside. 'It doesn't look like any of his friends are coming back for him,' she calls over her shoulder. 'In fact, I can't see a ghost town at all!'

The Doctor holds up his hands. 'Can we please stop calling it a 'ghost town' now? It's obviously not populated by spirits, is it?' He points at the unconscious creature at his feet.

'Yeah, but it's still pretty catchy,' Rory says.

'Can we please get back to the matter at hand?' Mr Azzopardi interjects. 'We have a... thing in the middle of our café. And personally I think we should tie it up — could be a useful bargaining tool if that town decides to return.'

'Tie it up? Tie it up?' the Doctor shouts. 'I've never heard anything like this before in my life! Of course we shouldn't tie it up — we should be getting it a bandage; the poor thing's had a nasty bump on the head.'

'You know, now it's asleep, it does look almost... cute,' Mrs Azzopardi adds from the far corner of the room, much to the astonishment of her husband.

If you agree with Mr Azzopardi and want to tie up the creature, go to 22.

If you decide to try and nurse its wound, go to 23.

22

The Doctor stands out on the porch whilst you help Mr Azzopardi with the rope, hastily drawing up a chair on which to perch the unconscious creature — he doesn't want any part of this.

'I think you're just being careful, and that's a good thing,' Amy whispers reassuringly as she improvises a bandage around the large exoskeleton of the creature's head. 'If it turns out to be harmless, we can always let it go.'

'Guilty until proven innocent, eh, Amy?' the Doctor shouts from outside.

'They've been driving people from their own homes, Doctor! If that doesn't make you a bit of a monster, I don't know what does!' Amy replies angrily.

Rory and Mrs Azzopardi re-enter the café a moment later, and you look up in surprise: you hadn't seen them leave. 'We were just out getting some supplies,' Rory explains, 'although Mrs Azzopardi might have told a couple of her friends about our... discovery.'

From outside a low murmur is increasing to a loud clamour as a crowd of angry villagers descends upon the little café; the Doctor finds himself pushed to the edge of the porch as the colonists jostle for a good view of the monster.

'You came back pretty sharpish once the ghost town had left,' the Doctor sniffs. 'I should have known that no one can resist a good freak show.'

Go to 28.

You rush to the back of the café to find the owner's first aid kit and return with armfuls of bandages and disinfectants.

'Great stuff!' The Doctor grins, grabbing a handful of bottles and frowning to examine the labels. 'Although not having seen one of these creatures before, I don't know whether these will help it or poison it.' He shrugs. 'I guess we'll just have to patch it up as best we can.'

Mrs Azzopardi leaves with Rory to get a bucket of water to bathe the wound, returning a moment later surrounded by a gaggle of villagers.

'What did you bring them for?' Amy hisses at her husband as he walks sheepishly into the café. She nods in the direction of the throng of villagers outside as they jostle for a position in the doorway, trying to get a good view of the creature.

'Sorry,' Rory whispers back. 'Turns out Mrs Azzopardi is a bit of a gossip. Although it was only thanks to us wandering about and making so much noise that the rest of them realised it was safe to come out of hiding!'

The Doctor strides out onto the porch, arms held high to usher the crowd away from the door. 'Calm down folks, calm down! The poor creature will be awake in a moment and then we can try and sort this whole thing out!'

'Doctor!' Amy suddenly calls from inside. 'Never mind in a moment; I think it's waking up now!'

Go to 27.

You lower the teapot and let it drop to the floor. Amy looks at you in horror, then back to the Doctor.

But the creature doesn't attack. Instead, its deep black eyes hold the Doctor's gaze before it straightens up to full height, the top of its head scraping against the beams of the café ceiling. Its pincers snap and jitter for a second before a crackling voice emanates from the back of the creature's throat like a voice through a radio at full volume.

'Leave your colony tonight and we will not harm you. But if you stay, we will return and next time we will have murder in our hearts,' it croaks.

The room stands in complete silence for a moment, before the Doctor steps forward. 'No,' he states simply.

The creature looks at him with what seems like puzzlement and cocks its head.

'No,' he repeats. 'How dare you come into these people's homes, trash their things and scare them half to death? You have no right! Leave, now!' He pauses. 'And if you do ever dare to return, then I will come to your home. And if I do then I promise,' his voice lowers to a growl, 'that it will be you that's scared to death!'

You hold your breath, unsure as to how the monster will react.

But it says nothing, instead turning and walking back through the remains of the café door. Before it leaves it turns once again to address the Doctor. 'You have been warned,' it says.

'He's not getting away with that.' The Doctor is already sprinting out of the café. 'You three – with me!'

You don't need telling twice and you race out of the café door, across the porch and into the network of walkways that make up the colony. But the creature has vanished.

Go to 17.

'Over here!' Amy calls as you race between the narrow buildings in search of the noise. You catch up with her and a moment later the Doctor and Rory are brought to a halt behind you, staring at the scene in front of them.

One of the creatures is lying prone on the ground, trapped under the remains of a heavy wooden door. The cross beam above it has snapped and a shard of wood has lodged the door in place. It struggles weakly to free itself but its claws are clutching at thin air.

'Oh, the poor thing!' Amy's hand flies to her mouth.

But Rory laughs. 'Poor thing? Poor thing? It's been trapped whilst trying to smash up the colony! If you ask me, it got what it deserved!'

'Why don't we try and reserve judgement until we've heard its side of the story, eh?' says the Doctor, beckoning for you to come and join him at the other side of the door. He counts you down. 'Three, two, one, heave!'

Together you manage to slide the wooden slab to one side, revealing the long, thin body of the creature below. It turns its face towards you to reveal a mouth bristling with pincers and two large, deep black eyes set beneath a chitinous brow.

'Thank you,' its pincers croak weakly before it falls unconscious.

'Um, Doctor?' Amy joins in.

'Not now, Amy!' the Doctor says. 'We need to carry it back to the café and treat its wounds!'

'Just look,' she says. You both turn. Mr and Mrs Azzopardi are standing behind you, mouths hanging open at the sight of the monster.

'Good,' says the Doctor. 'You can help carry our patient!'

Go to 23.

Rory agrees with you. 'You're right; it sounds like a war cry to me. They've obviously not all left yet – we should get back to the café until it's safe.'

Ignoring the Doctor's grumbles you lead the way, retracing your steps through the narrow alleyways. Suddenly Amy puts a hand on your arm, making you stop short. 'Wait,' she says.

The noisy clump of footsteps is approaching from a nearby walkway, accompanied by a rough, dragging sound from somewhere around the corner. You look for a place to hide, but it's too late.

Two figures appear from a side-passage and the Doctor is surprised to find that it's Mr and Mrs Azzopardi! 'What are you two doing out here?' he asks.

'Doctor!' The old man grins. 'We got bored of hiding and decided to come out for a bit of a look-see now the action's died down, and you'll never guess what we found!'

With a thud he drops the large object he had slung over his shoulder onto the walkway, and it's then that you realise that it's one of the creatures!

The monster's mouth of bristling pincers and long, chipped claws that stand in place of fingers look oddly pathetic as it lies unconscious. Its spindly limbs are tied tightly to its armoured body with a thick length of rope and the black shell-plates of the creature's torso make a soft grating noise as they move against each other in time with its breathing.

'I reckon this will help us 'persuade' our attackers to back off,' Mr Azzopardi continues triumphantly, straightening his tie.

'Either that, or get you all killed when they come back for it,' the Doctor scowls.

The old man shrugs, 'Suit yourself, Doctor, but we're taking it back to the café until it wakes up!'

Go to 22.

'Okay, everybody quiet!' the Doctor yells. 'I think it's time for talking, not gawping, now. Thank you!'

The Doctor drops to his haunches in front of the creature, smiling gently as it blinks its eyes and breathes deeply. 'It's okay,' he whispers, 'you're safe now. Well, sort of – but I think these angry villagers can wait to hear what you have to say before passing any kind of judgement.'

The creature sniffs and looks around cautiously at the roomful of faces. You give the monster your most reassuring of smiles and listen intently as it begins to speak.

'My name is Krane, and I am a Varna. Our species come from a planet not far from here, where we lived peacefully for centuries. But our sun was old and dying and we realised that we had to find a new home before it was extinguished completely. Unfortunately our technology for interstellar travel is not nearly as advanced as yours, and Betul was the only habitable planet that was within range of our ship.' Krane pauses, remembering the struggle his people endured. 'We meant no harm, and were quite happy to live on our floating town in the ocean. But soon word spread to the Galactic Council that we had changed addresses without permission and they warned us that if we didn't vacate the planet, they would send a Judoon squad to evict us. You got here first, you see.' He looks across the crowd of onlookers. 'So the land is yours by rights.'

'And now the Judoon have arrived,' the Doctor mutters. 'I knew it; it's always about the paperwork with those thugs.'

Krane nods. 'Indeed, but luckily another of our species, Teron, was well-versed in galactic law and discovered a clause in the small print of the settlement contract. He realised that if we could clear a big enough radius of uninhabited land around our city, we would be far enough away from your human colonies to be allowed to keep our modest town. Pressed for time, I'm afraid we resorted to scare tactics and sabotage to try and drive you away from us before the Judoon arrived. But sadly it appears that we are too late.'

The Doctor pats Krane gently on the shoulder and gets to his feet to address the crowd. 'You see?' he shouts. 'They're not monsters; they're simply another species like you, looking for a home!' He considers for a second. 'I admit that their tactics are a little... antisocial, but if you had the Judoon on your backs, trust me, you'd probably be doing the same!'

Amy looks at you and smiles. Rory, too, is grinning from ear to ear and you can't help but feel the mood in the room lift considerably.

'Now, how about we go down to the harbour and start some proper negotiations?'

Go to 29.

Mr Azzopardi has appointed himself head of the interrogation and now he steps up to the monster as it slowly opens its eyes. 'Good afternoon, sonny Jim,' the old man growls with a severity that surprises you. 'It must feel strange for you now that our roles are reversed, and it's me that's got the advantage over you!'

In response the creature strains at its bonds, pulling at the ropes in a violent fervour. Its pincers rattle as it lets out a crackling howl of anger. 'You won't get away with this!' it hisses. 'My people will come back, you'll see, and when they find out what you've done to me they'll kill every last one of you in cold blood!'

Mr Azzopardi seems unimpressed. 'Well, we will see! I've got a mind to escort you over to the harbour right now so that we can show your friends what we do with people who try to destroy our homes! And if they don't leave us alone and get off our planet right this instant, then they won't get you back! How does that sound?'

The crowd outside the café murmur their agreement as the Doctor looks around in horror at the angry mob that's beginning to form.

The creature renews its struggles once more, but this time it seems to realise the uselessness of the effort and slumps down in the chair, head resting against its black-ribbed chest.

Then it does something you hadn't expected. The monster begins to cry. Transparent green tears roll out of its large black eyes and begin to pool on the floorboards beneath it.

'Now look what you've done!' the Doctor says, pushing his way into the room. 'Just… give it a chance to speak, won't you?' He turns to you. 'Please?'

If you agree to let the monster try and explain, go to 27.

If you think that these monsters need to be confronted, go to 30.

Amy, Rory, the Doctor and yourself are at the head of the procession as it leads your new friend down to the harbour. Behind you, you can hear enthusiastic introductions and awkward handshakes as the colonists attempt to welcome their new guest.

You chuckle quietly as you hear Mrs Azzopardi suggest that the Varna might like to have a cake baked for their arrival and in no time at all you find yourself at the harbour. In front of you the fog has receded, exposing a calm ocean with a horizon that blends into a beautiful white haze.

Turning to the Doctor, you ask him what happens now.

'Well,' he says, shoving his hands in his pockets. 'I guess we wait for the Varna Village to return for their missing citizen.' There is a pause as the Doctor considers. '"Varna Village"... now I much prefer that to "ghost town", don't you?'

He checks his watch and his expression darkens suddenly. 'I hope they hurry up, though. I'd put bets on the Judoon sending over a scout force to check out the "locals" any moment now. I wonder who'll turn up first?'

A shiver runs down your spine as you stare into the glassy water ahead of you. Did it get a little colder all of a sudden?

Who will turn up first? If you have access to a computer, click on box C on screen and enter the code word GUESTS.

If you do not, toss a coin! Heads, go to 31. Tails, go to 32.

The procession that leads the monstrous prisoner down to the harbour has a funereal air to it, and the Doctor follows the mob in an angry silence.

Rory puts a comforting hand on your shoulder as you walk. 'I'm sure you did the right thing,' he says. 'At least, I hope you did.'

Once you reach the jetty, you watch with a sinking feeling as the bound prisoner is pushed along the walkway like a man walking the plank. 'Our cards are on the table,' Mr Azzopardi declares. 'Now the ball is in their court.'

Silence falls on the gathering, and grey mist drifts ominously across the still water of the ocean. The Doctor looks at his watch nervously and you ask him why.

'This is not a good situation to confront anybody with,' he explains reluctantly. 'But I can't predict what'll be worse: if these creatures return for their missing comrade and find him a prisoner or...' He trails off.

'Or what?' Amy asks.

'Or if the Judoon decide that now would be a good time to intervene,' he finishes. 'And if I know the Judoon, then the worst time to arrive is almost always the exact time they choose to show up.'

Who will turn up first? If you have access to a computer, click on box C on screen and enter the code word THREATS.

If you do not, toss a coin! Heads, go to 49. Tails, go to 50.

Imposing, armour-clad figures disembark from their landing craft and troop onto the jetty in sinister formation, the wood creaking under their hefty boot-heels.

'Amy, Rory – meet the Judoon,' the Doctor mutters.

Mr Azzopardi is confused. 'Wait, you're not the Varna. What on Betul are you?'

'Bo Ro Lo Fo Sho,' a gruff voice chants from beneath the heavy black helmet of the leader. He reaches to his belt, pulling a small crimson device from one of the slots and holds it up to Mr Azzopardi's worried face. There is a squeal as the device plays back the old man's speech and then the Judoon quickly jams it into a connector on the front of his armour.

'Language assimilated,' he states, before reaching up a pair of thickly gloved hands and easing off his helmet.

The crowd gasp at the alien features beneath. 'You didn't tell me they looked like giant space biker-rhinos,' Amy says to the Doctor.

'I keep forgetting the human need for comparisons to familiar creatures,' the Doctor responds.

As the crowd moves back, Krane steps forward to greet the new arrivals. 'Greetings, Judoon,' he says softly, his pincers clicking politely. 'As you can see, I have made contact with the human colonists and they have agreed to try and work out a way to co-exist with my

Varna cousins once they return for me.'

The Judoon looks at Krane, then at the crowd. Its eyes fix on you with a penetrating stare, as if sure that you are guilty of something – it just doesn't know what.

'No,' it says finally. 'The law is clear; your past behaviour is not acceptable.'

'We can change! These humans will forgive us.' Desperation is creeping into Krane's voice and he is supported by a murmur of agreement from the colonists.

But the Judoon ignores his pleas. 'You will come with us as our prisoner.'

'No!' Mr Azzopardi shouts. 'You can't do that. We are willing to settle this dispute and overcome our differences.'

'Do not argue with the law, human,' the leader responds.

Mr Azzopardi looks around nervously for support and catches your eye.

If you agree with Mr Azzopardi and want to defy the Judoon, go to 33.

If you think it's safer to hand over Krane rather than argue, go to 34.

With a familiar crunch the floating deck of the Varna Village connects with the jetty, and a horde of Varna emerge from their shelter amongst the ramshackle houses on board. Dark shapes flit over the rooftops before uncurling themselves onto the deck in front of the waiting humans.

'Krane,' the oldest of the Varna whispers hoarsely. His pincers are pale and thin and his shell is a mottled grey. 'What is the meaning of this? We thought that you had surely died at the hands of these humans.'

Krane steps forward, brushing away Mrs Azzopardi as she offers to support him. 'No, Teron. Thanks to the help of the Doctor and his friends, these colonists have heard of our plight and are prepared to help us settle the matter with the Judoon.'

Teron walks forward to grasp his comrade's claw with relief and looks around at the proud faces standing before him. 'I thought that humans were selfish, territorial savages. Obviously I was wrong.'

The Doctor steps in, raising a hand in greeting. 'They can be, Teron, but you should always give them a chance before assuming the worst!'

'I agree with you, Doctor, maybe we were too hasty.'

'Oh, not to worry.' The Doctor grins, shoving his hands in his pockets. 'All's well that ends well. Now that you lot have all decided to get along swimmingly at last, we just need to tie up some loose ends – well, one loose end, and that would be the Judoon.'

'More aliens?' Mr Azzopardi looks shocked. 'I'm not sure I can handle another menagerie of creatures… no offence.' He looks to the Varna.

'That is understandable,' Krane smiles. 'I believe that we can conduct our explanations elsewhere and meet the Judoon out at sea if you do not wish to have more unexpected guests.'

The Doctor looks worried. 'But you'll need someone to vouch for you, surely? Otherwise the Judoon are hardly likely to believe you.'

Teron looks at the Doctor. 'That is kind of you to offer, Doctor, but we Varna are a trustworthy race. I'm sure the Judoon will accept our story.'

If you want to leave the Varna to conduct their negotiations alone out at sea, go to 36.

If you and the Doctor decide to accompany them to make sure things run smoothly, go to 37.

You refuse to hand over Krane, and Mr Azzopardi looks relieved, mouthing a quick 'thank you' over his shoulder before confronting the Judoon.

'No, Krane stays with us and we will all wait here together until the Varna Village returns. We don't need your help; we can work it out ourselves.'

'This planet is under the jurisdiction of the Galactic Council. It is our job to enforce the law, not yours to work your way around it. If you get in our way, you will all be under arrest.' The Judoon leader will not be moved. It reaches out to grab Krane from the clutches of Mrs Azzopardi, but the Doctor leaps in between!

'Wait, wait, let's not do that — can't you see that Krane here is a victim, not a criminal? He and his people only wanted somewhere to live, and it was only because of your petty planning regulations that they were driven to attack the colonies. Can't you see that it was you that forced them to break the law?'

He glances around at Krane, who smiles nervously — his black eyes are large and wide and you can see the fear welling up inside him.

'No exceptions,' The Judoon insists. 'Stand aside or we will arrest you, too.'

'If you arrest the Doctor, then you'll have to arrest me as well!' Suddenly Amy is standing at the Doctor's side and Rory comes to join her, too.

'And me,' he adds.

You decide that it's time to take a stand and step forward to join the trio, forming a barrier across the jetty that divides the humans from the Judoon.

There is silence for a few moments whilst the Judoon considers this. 'Very well,' it says at last. 'You are all under arrest.'

You have a sinking feeling in the pit of your stomach and look to the Doctor to see if he has any ideas as to what to do next, but he too appears worried. Finally you turn to the colonists who are standing open-mouthed in silence behind you. In the midst of them is Krane, a tear rolling down his face. You look at the group with pleading eyes; will they help you or not?

The click of handcuffs makes you jump and, looking down, you realise that one of the Judoon has fastened them over your hands and is preparing to lead you back to their landing craft along with the Doctor, Amy and Rory. It's now or never.

If Mr Azzopardi decides to step forward, go to 41.

If he is too scared of putting the other colonists in danger, click on box D on screen and enter the code word PRISONER – or go to 38.

Reluctantly Mr Azzopardi steps aside. 'He's right.' He shoots a sad glance at the Doctor, registering the disappointment on the Time Lord's face. 'We should obey the law and have faith that it will resolve this issue legally and do the right thing.'

He turns gently to his wife, who is gripping Krane's arm. 'Honey, let go of the alien monster please so that the other alien monsters can deal with him.'

'Are you sure this is the right thing to do?' she asks him fearfully.

'I hope so,' he replies, leading Krane over to the Judoon captain. You watch Mrs Azzopardi wince as the cuffs snap closed over the creature's spindly arms.

Before he can board the Judoon craft, Krane turns to look over at the crowd, and a tear runs down his face. 'Thank you, Doctor, the Azzopardis, Amy, Rory – and you most of all.' He nods in your direction. 'For I fear that this might be goodbye.'

'What does he mean, Doctor? The Judoon will sort it out now that they know how things have changed, won't they?' Amy asks quietly.

'I've met the Judoon many times, Amy,' the Doctor says slowly, watching the hatch on the landing craft close with a soft hiss and clunk of metal. 'But never once have I seen one change its mind.'

Go to 35.

Sean the fisherman is the only colonist left in the harbour by the time the Doctor finally decides to speak. He is perched on a fence post with a mud-caked pair of waders in his lap, polishing them vigorously in an attempt to avoid the accusing eyes of your group.

The Judoon landing craft have long since disappeared into the mists with its prisoner.

'Well, I guess that's that,' the Doctor sighs.

'They're policemen, not murderers, Doctor,' Rory answers in an attempt to comfort him. 'I'm sure they won't do anything hasty.'

The Doctor looks at Rory with steely eyes. 'But what those creatures did was illegal in the Judoon's eyes. And the Galactic Council have a zero tolerance policy on behaviour like that.'

He pauses, breathing deeply in an attempt to bury his rage. 'The Judoon looked more like a clean-up squad than a group of investigators. They weren't interested in anything we had to say.'

Amy puts an arm around him. 'Time will tell, Doctor. There's nothing we can do now. Let's get back in the dry, have another cup of tea and just wait and see what happens.'

Together you walk slowly out of the harbour and back to the café.

Go to 39.

You stand on the shoreline as the Varna Village moves slowly out to sea. Krane's silhouette fades away as the mist swallows him up.

'Do you think we should have stayed on board?' the Doctor asks you, pulling his jacket closer in the sudden chill. 'If they confront the Judoon with no evidence that the colonists are willing to cooperate, they're just going to sound desperate.'

Amy steps forward. 'I know it's not exactly in your nature to just leave things alone and see what happens, Doctor, but the humans and Varna are both civilised and intelligent races. Maybe we should leave them to make their own decisions and mistakes.'

The Doctor sniffs and turns away. He solemnly treads the wooden boards as he heads back to the colony, with the rest of you trailing behind. You catch up with him and ask him what the matter is — maybe Amy's right?

'You don't know the Judoon,' he responds. 'They don't let people make mistakes. You get one chance with them, that's it, and if you mess it up...' he trails off and looks out to sea once more before shaking his head and dismissing the notion. 'But it's too late to worry now. Let's just go and get some tea.'

You exchange insincere smiles and walk back to the café. Rory pulls his jacket over his head as a cool drizzle begins to cover everything with a glossy sheen.

Go to 39.

'I'm glad you decided to come along,' Krane says to you. The Varna Village is disembarking from the harbour, the black sails unfurling and catching the breeze as you head out to sea. 'I didn't want to impose on the colonists, but the Judoon have been known to be rather... unreasonable sometimes.'

'Well, they won't be able to get away with any funny business whilst we're here,' Rory interrupts. 'The Doctor won't let them.'

You look over at the Doctor, who is talking animatedly with Teron. The other Varna have gathered around, listening in on the exchange with animated curiosity, their pincers clacking gently.

Out at sea the mist is bitingly cold, and Amy is stomping up and down the deck in an attempt to keep warm. Rory walks over to her, wrapping his jacket around her comfortingly. You hope that everything will be okay.

'Judoon sighted!' comes a cry from the lookout post on the roof of the tallest stack of dwellings. The village falls silent as everyone turns to scour the mists, black eyes searching for the Judoon landing craft.

Suddenly a dark shape looms alongside — a large metal landing craft. Its front hatch descends and a troop of black, armour-clad creatures emerge, the deck rocking as their stomping boots board the village.

The leader removes his helmet to reveal a large, rhino-like head, and its breath puffs into clouds of condensation as it snarls. It produces a small crimson device from its belt and holds it out to the astonished group.

The Doctor steps forward. 'Hello, Judoon,' he speaks into the piece.

'Language assimilated,' the Judoon states. 'You are all under arrest.'

Go to 40.

A few moments later you are escorted to a cell on the lowest deck of the towering Judoon ship. It is cold and suffocating and a tiny porthole displays a dark view of the undersea landscape of Betul. You turn at the sound of the Doctor being pushed inside behind you.

'You're making a big mistake!' the Doctor shouts at the impassive guard as he slams the huge iron door closed with an echoing clang. 'I'm the Doctor! The Shadow Proclamation will have something to say about this!'

But the sound of stomping feet is already disappearing down the corridor outside and you realise that you are quite alone. You ask the Doctor if there is anything he can do – some way of escaping this prison. But the Doctor is silent and fiddles awkwardly with his bow tie. Finally he gets out his sonic screwdriver and shines the soft green light around the edges of the door.

'Nope, as I suspected, it's all double-deadlocked, and why not? The Judoon have the strongest holding cells in the galaxy.' He sighs and looks at you. 'I'm afraid there's no way out, we're stuck here, and it's a long journey to the Galactic Council.'

There is a low rumble from beneath your feet and, looking out of the porthole, you see the surface of the water crash past you as the ship lifts off into the sky. The atmosphere of Betul flashes by and soon you are confronted with the empty blackness of space.

You slump roughly to the floor and rest your head against the cold grey wall behind you. This wasn't how you'd imagined your adventures with the Doctor would end.

THE END

The café porch is both familiar and strange as you sit at your old table amongst the shards of wood and broken crockery that litter the floor. From inside the café you can hear the fussy sounds of Mrs Azzopardi as she potters around with a mop, and you feel slightly guilty that you're sitting outside drinking tea with nothing to do.

The Doctor taps the table absent-mindedly with a finger. He looks around with anxiety, his tea untouched and going cold in front of him, whilst Amy and Rory chat loudly in an attempt to get you both to relax.

Suddenly the horizon glows bright yellow and orange and the mist evaporates immediately in the accompanying heat wave to reveal a huge ball of fire rising slowly over the sea.

You leap to your feet and run to the balcony, Amy and Rory appearing next to you. As you watch, flaming debris and wood begin to descend through the clouds, hissing loudly as the sea extinguishes them. You don't need to guess what they are the remains of.

'The Varna...' Amy trails off.

'All gone,' says the Doctor, still sitting at the table. His hand shakes with barely contained grief as he raises the cup to his lips and takes a sip. 'Resisting arrest, no doubt.'

He gets up to leave, wiping his hands with a napkin. 'Time to go home, I think,' he says, looking at you. 'I'm sorry that I wasn't able to give you a happy ending.'

He turns his sad eyes to Rory and Amy, who nod quietly. Then he screws up the napkin and walks forlornly back to the TARDIS.

THE END.

'Wait, wait, wait.' The Doctor takes a deep breath and holds a hand up to halt the advancing squad of Judoon. 'Just listen to them! They've talked with the colonists and believe that they can resolve their differences. Give them a chance to speak.'

The Judoon leader looks at the Doctor with a sneer, before batting his hand away like a fly. 'Are you a colonist?' it asks gruffly.

The Doctor starts to fiddle with his cuffs. 'Well, no. But some of my best friends are...' he trails off.

'If you are not a colonist, you are irrelevant,' the Judoon snaps.

'Hey, hold on a minute,' Rory joins in. 'We're witnesses and we're telling you that the colonists and the Varna are willing to come to an agreement. Tell 'em Krane!'

Krane steps forward. 'We are — you must believe us! I know that we have broken the law, but we had no choice. We beg you to give us a chance.'

'Like all criminals, you lie.' The captain will not be moved.

'Just go back to the colony and talk to the humans,' Amy pleads. 'It can't hurt to give them the benefit of the doubt.'

'Criminals have no right to the "benefit of the doubt".' The Judoon pushes past you and into the centre of the deck. 'Judoon, take care of these squatters according to Galactic Law.'

As one, the Judoon squad raise their guns.

Go to 45.

'Ahem!' A loud cough makes the Judoon swing around. Mr Azzopardi has stepped forward and is shaking like a leaf. 'Um, you see,' he stumbles over his words, 'what I'm trying to say is, that you either arrest all of us, or none of us.'

The Judoon captain stomps over to him angrily. 'And you speak for all the colonists?' he growls.

The old man wipes the sweat from his brow before looking at his wife who returns his gaze with a reassuring nod.

'Yes.' He straightens up, more confident now. 'Yes, I do. So, er, Judoon, what's it going to be?'

'Mr Azzopardi, I am so proud of you!' the Doctor yells over his wardens' heads. Ducking beneath their burly arms he runs over to the old man, shaking his hand firmly, despite the cuffs. 'That's all I needed! I can take it from here.'

He swings around to face the Judoon captain. 'Right, Judoon captain, these fellows might not know anything about Galactic Law but I certainly do. From what I've read of the small print, I seem to remember it stating something about cataloguing all suspects before arrest, does it not?'

The Judoon Leader's face falls and he raises an angry fist. You flinch, worried that he's about to attack the Doctor, but realise that he is actually signalling to his men. 'The law must be obeyed,' the

Judoon commands. 'Catalogue these humans.'

Immediately the soldiers fan out amongst the crowd, conducting quick retinal scans and marking off the colonists one by one. You sidle over to the Doctor and ask what he's doing.

'Buying us some time,' he whispers back. 'If I can keep the Judoon occupied for long enough then maybe... Aha!' He points over your shoulder and you look around.

Tearing through the clinging strands of mist is the Varna Village, heralding its arrival with an agitated chattering of Varna as they spot the Judoon landing craft.

Krane runs forward to greet the alien leader as he hauls himself onto the jetty; he is old and his shell is mottled, but you can see he still has life in his large eyes.

'Teron, I have contacted the colonists and I believe that we can work out a solution,' Krane says. 'But we need to work together quickly before the Judoon can arrest us all!'

Go to 43.

You explain to the Doctor that you think, for safety's sake, everybody should stay in one place and wait for the Judoon to arrive.

'Good call,' the Doctor responds. 'This way we can lay everybody's motives out on the table, and the Judoon won't be able to accuse the Varna of lying if the colonists are here to vouch for them.' He grins and rubs his hands. 'Right, well I suppose at the moment all we have to do is wait!'

You look around at the throng of humans and aliens as they begin to mill around, greeting each other for the first time, and you feel proud. Amy appears beside you and smiles.

'It's a great feeling, isn't it, knowing that you're putting things right? That's why I love travelling with the Doctor.'

'Oi, look sharp, I think someone's about to crash our little party!' Rory shouts from his position at the end of the jetty.

The Doctor leaps over to him, followed closely by you and Amy. Out of the mist, a dark metal shape is approaching – a heavy steel ship with a large hatch at the front that makes it look like a bulldozer.

'A Judoon landing craft,' the Doctor murmurs. 'We didn't have to wait long.'

With a loud crunch the ship grinds to a halt at the shoreline, the hatch slamming open onto the wet mulch, and the Judoon squad tramps into the harbour. The captain removes his helmet as he approaches

Teron and Mr Azzopardi, who have stopped mid-handshake to stare at the newcomers.

His squat face and horned nose wrinkle into a snarl as he surveys the crowd in front of him. 'Explain what is going on here!' he roars loudly.

Go to 43.

The harbour divides neatly into thirds as the three races separate and confront each other. A heavy silence descends on the harbour, broken only when the footsteps of the Doctor begin to echo around the wooden slats as he makes his way to the centre of the make-shift arena.

'Well,' he says loudly. 'Well, well, well, well, well.' There is a pause as he considers for a second. 'Well.' He finishes. He looks to Amy as if asking for a prompt.

'You're negotiating!' Amy hisses to him.

'Oh yes!' the Doctor remembers. He spreads his arms and addresses the menagerie of creatures before him. 'Judoon, Varna and humans, lend me your ears! Except maybe for the Varna, who don't have ears as such, more a kind of developed sonar thingy...'

'Get on with it!' Rory heckles.

'Sorry.' The Doctor turns to the Judoon. 'Okay, you first. Whilst you were away, the Varna and the humans appear to have got over their little disagreement and now that they have explained their situation, the colonists are willing to accept the Varna as neighbours and forgive their past crimes.'

'The law does not forgive,' the Judoon captain snaps.

'The law is designed to keep the peace, Captain! And I don't care what your rulebook says — you slapping cuffs on everybody isn't going to achieve that.' The Judoon is speechless and the Doctor flashes him a disarming grin. 'But you know what? I might have just the thing to keep all three of you lovely races happy.'

Slowly he reaches a hand behind his back and, with a flourish and accompanying 'tadaa!' he produces a mysterious wad of papers. The crowd move closer...

Go to 44.

You all gather round, pressing in to see what the Doctor is holding. He gives you a reassuring grin and hands the wad of papers to you.

'Would you be so good as to distribute these amongst everybody?' he asks.

You take the sheaf of papers and glance at the header. It reads: 'For the Granting of Planning Permission on Offworld Colonies'.

But before you can take a closer look, the crowd descends upon you, eager to take a form, and you begin to hand out the papers to humans and Varna alike. A hush falls on the assembly as the people begin to read and the Doctor hops onto a nearby post to explain.

'What you have in your hands is a planning permission form: a legal document that, once filled in, will legally allow both races to live in peace on Betul. If the humans could sign the section that says "As a neighbour of this new settlement I am happy to allow the construction to take place" and if the Varna could sign the paragraph that says "I promise to respect my neighbours and abide by the terms of their agreement", then that would be just hunky dory!' He turns to the Judoon captain. 'And Captain, if you and your men could avoid arresting or shooting anybody long enough for them to sign it then I would be eternally grateful!'

With a curt grunt the Judoon captain nods and places his hands on his hips as he inspects the excited citizens with keen eyes.

'Um,' says a confused voice in the crowd. You spot a small hand waving from the back of the excited throng. 'Has anybody got a pen?'

There is a murmur of confusion for a second as everyone checks their pockets and the Doctor's face falls, suddenly worried that his plan might be about to fall apart.

Luckily, at the last minute, a triumphant shout goes up. It's Sean the fisherman!

'I have one! Always keep it handy for signing my boat in and out.'

A sigh of relief erupts around you and you find yourself unwittingly joining in as order is restored once more. One by one the humans and Varna hand you back the completed forms and you shuffle them together before handing them to the Judoon captain. He frowns at you as he takes the papers and you can smell his stinking breath as he begins to rifle through the pile, studying each one in turn.

'I hope everyone filled it in correctly. One mistake and we could all be in trouble,' the Doctor whispers.

Go to 46.

'No incineration,' the Judoon captain commands. 'These bystanders need not be harmed. Take the Varna to the cells.'

'What are you going to do with them?' Amy asks nervously.

'We will transport them to the Grobar Penal Colony,' he replies. 'The sentence is life imprisonment.'

You ask the Doctor what he's talking about.

'The Grobar Penal Colony is the most infamous prison in the quadrant,' he explains. 'A grotty, unpleasant mess where the inmates barely sleep, toiling for days in the mines beneath the complex.'

The cold tone of his voice sends a shiver down your spine and you wonder how such brutal a punishment could be inflicted on such a peaceful species.

'The Judoon obey the law to the letter and inflict the maximum penalty on all criminals in the hope that it will persuade future offenders to rethink their actions. But the Varna don't deserve this; they're innocent and willing to compromise – we have to do something!'

It's then that you realise the Doctor is looking to you to make the right move.

'You wanted to travel with us,' he says simply. 'Sometimes, to do what's right, we have to put ourselves in danger.'

A ripple of snapping cuffs cuts through the damp atmosphere as the Judoon begin to arrest the Varna, and you realise that it's now or never.

If you think that protesting now would be a futile gesture, go to 48.

If you decide that now is the time to prove your worth, go to 47.

Eventually the captain simply nods and hands the forms to one of the other soldiers for filing. 'Everything is in order,' he growls. 'The Varna may stay.'

Krane throws his head back and howls an alien shout of triumph before giving Teron and Mrs Azzopardi a hug, their smiles echoed by the rest of the crowd.

'Careful,' says Mr Azzopardi with a cheeky grin. 'Any more of that and we might file a noise complaint against our neighbours!'

One of the Judoon steps forward, and the old man holds up his palms quickly.

'It was a joke. A joke!' he insists.

You walk over to join the Doctor at the end of one of the jetties, where the Judoon are boarding their landing craft once more.

'So, no hard feelings then, eh?' you hear him say, slapping the captain on the back.

'Feelings are irrelevant in these circumstances,' the captain responds. 'The law has been obeyed.'

'Thank you for giving them the chance.' The Doctor smiles.

The celebrations are already beginning as the craft slips quietly away into the fog and you walk back towards the town with the Doctor. The evening sky is set alight with a rainbow of fireworks as the two races party through the streets of the colony. Even Amy and Rory are having fun, hands linked in a circle with Mr and Mrs Azzopardi, as a choir of Varna warble a tune for them to dance to.

The Doctor rests a hand on your shoulder. 'And thank you,' he says, 'for having faith.' He's beaming with pride.

'Right!' he declares suddenly, clapping his hands together. 'I think our work here is done. Time to be moving on I think.'

'But the party's only just beginning,' you point out.

'And we should let them party without us; the Varna and humans are celebrating a new relationship – it's their night, not ours.' He waves to Amy and Rory, who kiss the Azzopardis quickly on the cheeks before running over.

'Time to leave?' asks Amy. The Doctor nods.

'We're not taking our friend home already, are we?' Rory looks at you, crestfallen.

'I'm afraid so...' the Doctor winks at you. 'But I'm sure we could always take the scenic route. The TARDIS can be a little unpredictable at times, so who knows what adventures we might have along the way!'

Amy steps forward and shakes your hand enthusiastically.

'Welcome aboard!' she says.

THE END

You shake your head. The Judoon have made up their minds. You'd only be making trouble for Amy and Rory if you caused a fuss now and your friends come first. The Doctor blinks and looks away, eyes filled with disappointment.

Silently, the squad lead their prisoners one by one onto the waiting landing craft and you hang your head in shame as Teron and Krane are escorted past. A moment later the hatch of the landing craft hisses shut and it turns in the water, heading out to sea in the direction of the Judoon ships. The wood of the village groans around you as the barrels beneath rock in its wake and soon silence descends once more.

Rory goes to sit on a small crate next to where Amy has perched herself and heaves his legs out in front of him, glad to take the weight off his feet.

'At least the humans are safe,' he declares flatly, putting his arm around Amy as you turn and walk away.

You find the Doctor standing alone in the lookout post at the top of the village and touch his arm to make your presence known as he stares mournfully out to sea. But the Doctor ignores you, instead heaving a great sigh.

'Right,' he says finally. 'It's about time we sent you home. Maybe next time I'll think twice before taking someone for a ride in my ship.'

Slowly he unravels the huge coiled ropes on either side of the lookout post and begins to heave open the large black sails of the village. They flap loudly for a few seconds before the wind catches them and pulls them tight. With a great creaking and swaying the ghost town begins to move through the still water once more, heading back to the shore, and the TARDIS.

THE END

You are filled with a burning desire not to let the Doctor down; if you're going to earn your place in his TARDIS then you need to do something. You step out in front of the Judoon captain, blocking his route to the landing craft, and hold out your hand to stop him.

The captain stomps to a halt in front of you, his stinking breath filling your nostrils and making you want to gag.

'Do you protest?' he growls softly.

You nod slowly, looking over his shoulder to the Doctor.

'Yes, he protests!' the Doctor shouts, coming to your aid. 'We all do! Your treatment of the Varna is outrageous!'

Rory sinks his head into his hands. 'It's always got to be all of us, hasn't it?'

'I wouldn't have it any other way.' Amy gets to her feet, jaw set in defiance. 'Of course we protest, how could we not?'

The captain is silent for a moment, considering carefully before finally uttering one word. 'Good.'

The Doctor looks uncertain. 'Good? What do you mean, good? I don't like it when people say 'good'!'

The Judoon holds up a hand for silence and clears his booming throat.

'If you protest, then I can charge you with obstruction of justice. Guards! Arrest them all; they are no longer innocent bystanders, they are criminals.'

A huge pair of iron cuffs are fastened around your wrists and you find yourself herded into the landing craft along with the Varna.

'Thank you for trying to help us,' says Teron, 'but I fear that such an effort might have been in vain.'

If you have access to a computer, click on box D on screen and type in the code word PRISONER.

If you do not, go to 38.

The Doctor groans as the dark shadow of a Judoon landing craft pushes through the heavy mists. Its dirty steel bulk makes the walkways judder as it hits the edge of the jetty where the prisoner is bound, its head hunched into its shoulders.

'Trustworthy as ever, the Judoon.' The Doctor presents them to you as the front end of the craft splits open and huge, armour-clad beasts stomp onto the wooden jetty.

The captain of the squad removes his huge black helmet to reveal tough, leathery features and a horned nose. The crowd gasp in fear.

'How many monsters are lurking about out there?' Mr Azzopardi hisses to his wife, wincing suddenly as the captain shoves a small crimson device into his face and plugs it into a slot in his armour with a short hiss.

'Language assimilated.'

Mrs Azzopardi steps forward, trembling. 'What do you want?' she asks.

The captain holds up his hand and you flinch instinctively, but nothing happens. 'Do not fear us, humans; we are here to help you purge Betul of the Varna menace.'

Rory looks at you keenly. 'Good call, mate,' he says. 'Looks like a lot of people out there agree with you.'

'It's all a matter of perspective,' the Doctor snaps. 'Just because they're the law, doesn't mean the Judoon always get things right.'

'Well, from where I'm standing, Doctor, these 'Varna' don't make a very good first impression. It's not like they didn't have the chance,' Rory says indignantly.

The Doctor huffs and shoves his hands into his pockets. Mr Azzopardi motions you over and together you drag the tied-up monster over to the Judoon captain. The beast turns its head slowly and as you see yourself reflected in its deep black eyes, a sudden guilt washes over you.

'It's too late to back out now.' Mr Azzopardi notices that you've stopped. 'It's not our problem any more.'

The huge soldiers lift the creature out of your hands and throw him into the back of the landing craft.

'Thank you for your cooperation,' the captain grunts. 'Soon this planet will be yours again.'

At the last moment you cautiously tap the Judoon's arm and ask what will happen to the Varna now.

'The law is clear on the sentence for squatters,' the Judoon states. 'The punishment will fit the crime.'

With a loud clank and hiss of hydraulics, the hatch descends once more and the ship begins to disembark. You turn to face the crowd of onlookers, avoiding the Doctor's gaze as Mr Azzopardi addresses the hoard of frightened faces.

'The alien menace is over. We can all sleep soundly in our beds once again.'

A half-hearted cheer breaks the silence and Mrs Azzopardi runs over to embrace her husband. Realising that the action is over, the crowd begins to disperse as you are joined by Amy and Rory.

'Well, we've saved another group of humans from an alien menace. Not bad for your first trip aboard the TARDIS.' Rory winks at you.

'Yeah,' Amy agrees quietly, looking over to where the Doctor is kicking at a grassy tuft between planks. 'So why aren't we celebrating?'

Go to 35.

The sprawling hulk of the ghost town crunches into the side of the harbour with all the grace of a cannonball. The colonists crane their necks to see into the dark spaces between the cramped buildings as a huge chattering erupts from the shadows.

The imprisoned creature stands silently on the jetty in front of you and you feel a sudden fear at his lack of movement.

'This is going to get a little tense,' the Doctor warns you.

You peer into the gloom and suddenly realise that the shadows are filled with the huge black eyes of the alien townsfolk. One by one they lope out into the light and Amy squeezes your arm as their hideous bodies glisten with the moisture of the atmosphere.

'What have you done to Krane?' hisses a mottled monster, lifting a clawed hand and pointing to your prisoner. The humans remain silent.

Mr Azzopardi turns to you. 'Well, I suppose it was our call,' he urges. 'Looks like it's going to have to be us that do the talking.'

Hesitantly, you step forward, drawing yourself up as tall as possible as the creatures swarm in front of you.

'We have, uh, 'Krane' here as our prisoner.' Mr Azzopardi starts, his voice trembling as the monster looms over him. 'We are sick and tired of your alien ghost ship terrorising our colonies, and we demand that you stop, or else…'

'Or else what?' the monster hisses aggressively.

'Or else there's going to be trouble,' Mr Azzopardi finishes.

'There's going to be a lot more than trouble if you do not let our comrade go. There will be violence, revenge and bloodshed tonight if you do not back away immediately.'

You can see Mr Azzopardi trembling. He falters, but refuses to move. 'I will not step back, sir, until I have your word—' He flinches as the creature's claw snaps upward, poised to strike!

'Wait!' The cry makes everyone stop in their tracks. 'I will not stand by and let two intelligent races declare war on each other!' You turn to see the Doctor, striding along the jetty. You flash him a relieved smile, thankful that he has decided to step forward once more, but he ignores you.

'No, we will stop and we will wait and we will not move, until we have sorted this sorry mess out.' He perches himself awkwardly on a nearby post and folds his arms. 'Right.' He gives a wry smile. 'Shall we begin?'

Do you let the Doctor have his say? If so, go to 51.

If you think the colonists should negotiate for themselves, go to 52.

Mr Azzopardi clears his throat but you nudge him, finger to your lips, and nod in the direction of the Time Lord. Maybe he should have his say. The Doctor raises an eyebrow at you, then nods graciously before getting to his feet.

'Okay, firstly, to what species am I talking, please?' he asks politely.

The mottled monster steps forward cautiously.

'We are the Varna and I am Teron, leader of our village.'

The Doctor runs an exasperated hand through his hair. 'Thank you, Teron. I'm the Doctor.' He points an accusing finger. 'You know, I must say that for a leader you have shown very poor judgement in this situation.'

'Humans find our appearance repulsive. We have never had the chance to explain ourselves, and when we spotted the Judoon ships arriving from the stars, we realised that we had little time left. It is true that we have resorted to primitive violence, but we had no choice; the Judoon wish to evict us from Betul and our race hasn't the capacity to leave now that we have settled.'

'Well, I can see how the possibility of eviction at the hands of the Judoon can drive people to such lengths. They're not a gentle species.'

'Then you understand our plight, Doctor?'

'I understand it, but I don't approve of your actions. I think in different circumstances we might have managed to create some sort of peace between the two colonies, but look at what you have done to the humans now.' He gestures around the frightened crowd. 'You've made them suspicious and aggressive; there's no friendship to be formed here. The best I can suggest is that I find you an alternative world for your town; maybe there you won't make the same mistake.'

Teron bows his head in shame. 'Anything to avoid the punishment of the Judoon. I accept your terms, Doctor.'

'And in the nick of time as well.' Amy points. 'Look who's coming to dinner!'

Go to 53.

Mr Azzopardi clears his throat and you motion to the Doctor to let the colonists have their say; it's their problem and they should be allowed the chance to sort it out for themselves.

'We will return Krane freely if you promise to leave and never bother us again,' he states finally.

You nudge him.

'Er, please,' he adds.

Teron tips his head to the side, considering for a moment. 'And we demand that you relocate your colony, away from our village. This planet is as much ours as it is yours.'

'But we got here first!' Mr Azzopardi retorts.

'And our home world is dead; we have no choice in where we must settle, let alone the means to relocate. The human race spans countless planets across the galaxy – grant us this one.'

'No.' The crowd turn suddenly, as a small figure pushes his way through the onlookers – a fisherman, Sean. 'You lost the right to negotiate with us when you trashed our homes and scared our families. You do not deserve to stay here; we have done nothing wrong and will not be intimidated.' He is shaking with rage, jabbing a chubby finger at the Varna as he speaks. A murmur of agreement ripples through the watching colonists and you realise that the negotiations are in danger of breaking down.

'Maybe we should stop this before a fight breaks out,' Amy whispers in your ear. 'Ask them to give the humans some space to think; let them calm down and recover from the raid – they'll never reach an agreement today after what's just happened.'

You agree, raising your hands to call for silence. Maybe both races need to pause for thought; even with the Judoon waiting in the wings, a peaceful agreement reached in time is surely better than war?

There is a moment's silence as both the Varna and colonists consider the suggestion, before finally Teron speaks.

'Hand over Krane and we will consider a compromise.'

'No way!' says Sean, affronted. 'The prisoner is our only bargaining chip; if we let it go then we'll be powerless!'

If you decide to release Krane, go to 54.

If you think the colonists should hold the creature until an agreement has been reached, go to 55.

Out of the fog looms the hulking shape of the Judoon landing craft, a massive steel box with a huge hatch that hisses and squeals on hydraulics as it lowers onto the creaking wooden boards.

The crowd step back as huge, lumbering figures stomp out of the gloomy interior. The leader of the squad removes his domed helmet to reveal a leathery, wrinkled face and a vicious, horned nose.

'Bo Ro Ho Ko Bo!' he grunts loudly as his troops fan out, gloved hands twitching eagerly by their holstered weapons. You flinch in fear as the stinking captain steps forward and you suddenly find a small crimson tube thrust towards your face.

'Speak into it,' the Doctor nudges you. 'It's a translation device.'

With a concerted effort, you manage to keep your voice steady long enough to introduce yourself. Satisfied, the captain plants the tube into a hole in his chest and after a short hiss he growls, 'Language assimilated.'

'Good stuff, good stuff.' The Doctor gives a brief clap of approval, immediately drawing the crowd's attention. 'So, now we've got the formalities out of the way, how about we tell you where we've got to?'

If the Judoon had an eyebrow, it would raise it.

'These Varna that you've come to arrest for trespassing, they're stuck here – they can't leave, no matter how many times you send them angry letters. And it's your intimidation that's forcing them to act aggressively towards their neighbours.'

'The law is the law,' the captain replies. 'It is not our problem if criminals cannot find transport.'

The Doctor draws himself up to his full height, straightening his bow tie and tossing his hair from his face. 'It is now,' he says grimly.

Go to 56.

As you move to untie the creature's bonds, Sean scowls and steps forward in an attempt to stop you. At the last minute the Doctor jumps in.

'A peaceful agreement can never be reached without trust. Using living, breathing people as bargaining chips is not the way forward, believe me.'

'He's right, Sean, step back. I'll not have you start a fight in our colony,' says Mr Azzopardi. Reluctantly, the fisherman retreats into the crowd.

Krane rubs at his limbs as the rope falls to the floor and he turns to you gratefully. 'You have made a wise decision today,' he says. 'This gesture bodes well for the future of our two races.'

The atmosphere of suspicion and mistrust is replaced with an audible sigh of relief as the Varna reluctantly return to their village. Teron wraps a claw around Krane to support him as he steps onto the gently shifting wooden deck of the vessel and turns to face the colonists for the last time.

'We will see you again,' he says.

Behind him the huge black sails of the town unfurl and the craft begins to pull away into the water until it is swallowed by the fog.

'Will you, I wonder?' the Doctor murmurs.

You ask what he means.

'If the Judoon are on the hunt for the Varna, then they won't be very keen to hang around and see what happens between the two races. To them justice is a dish best served swiftly and efficiently. Empty promises of compromise might not mean much to them.' He rubs his chin, deep in thought.

'Well, it's too late now, Doctor,' Rory points out. 'They're gone. The colony is safe.'

'Indeed, but I think we should stick around a little while longer... just in case.'

A cool breeze makes you shiver as you pick your way across the harbour with the rest of the colonists, back towards the café and the comforting warmth of the Azzopardis' tea.

Go to 39.

You agree with Sean: these monsters have already attacked the colony once and without a prisoner to bargain with, there's no guarantee they won't do so again. You lead the colonists as they move forward to surround Krane, a human barrier between him and the rest of his species.

'We are prepared to negotiate, but only from strength,' says Sean. 'The prisoner will stay with us until an agreement has been reached.'

Teron's pincers crack and snap with anger. 'We refuse to deal with blackmailers, human.' His voice lowers to a threatening whisper. 'You have proved that your kind is unworthy of the Varna's trust.'

With a snap Teron raises his claw and the Varna fan out on either side of their leader. The moisture in the air makes their black shells glisten in the low light and their huge eyes narrow as they prepare to fight for their captive comrade.

'Get the women and children away from here, quickly,' Mr Azzopardi hisses. 'We can't hope to hold them off for long.'

The colonists scream in panic, the crowd dispersing as the citizens make a break for shelter.

'Let the hunt begin,' Teron hisses.

As one the Varna begin to pace forward, eyes fixed on their prey, waiting for them to make one false move. Mr Azzopardi grabs your arm and pulls you back along the pier. 'I'm sorry it had to end this way,' he tells you. 'This wasn't what I wanted.'

'This wasn't what anyone wanted!' the Doctor yells. 'But it's too late now!'

You cover your eyes as the Varna prepare to pounce… is this the end?

Go to 57.

'What's he saying?' Rory hisses as Amy sits down next to you.

'I dunno, something about a Shadow Proclamation and having friends in high places. Then he started on about the lenience of the law or something.' She shrugs.

You're sitting with the couple on a nearby barrel as the Doctor talks with a quiet urgency to the Judoon captain. Teron lopes over to your group, never taking his eyes off the Doctor and the captain.

'Do you know what's happening? Are we to be arrested?' he asks with a nervous clatter of pincers.

You tell him his guess is as good as yours, and Teron nods slowly.

'Don't worry, Teron.' Amy puts a comforting hand against his mottled shell. 'The Doctor won't stand by and let a race be punished for something they couldn't avoid.'

'I hope you're right,' says Teron. 'The stories we hear about the Judoon...' he trails off as if the memory is too painful to recall.

Suddenly, the wait is over and the Doctor and the captain exchange a brief handshake before turning to face the frightened group of Varna.

'It's okay,' the Doctor says, holding up a calming hand. 'I've reminded the Judoon of the spirit of the law, and they have agreed that in these special circumstances they will make an exception.'

'Just this once,' the captain interjects.

'You will be transported on their ships as guests.' The Doctor gives the Judoon a hard stare. 'A word that isn't to be confused with prisoners the moment you leave my sight, may I add.' He turns his attention back to the Varna, 'And as guests you will be taken to a rather lovely little uninhabited planet that I know of near the Chapman Belt where you can start anew.'

He looks around in the silence that follows. 'Will that do?'

'Doctor, you have saved our people!' Teron exclaims, stepping forward. 'And for that we will be forever grateful. Fellow Varna, we have a new home!'

Go to 58.

A huge explosion knocks you off your feet and you're sent tumbling backwards across the jetty.

'I've got you.' Rory grabs your arm just in time to stop you falling into the icy water of the harbour. Dazed and confused, you look up to see the ghost town reduced to a splintered wreck. Huge orange flames billow from the closely-packed buildings and a cloud of thick black smoke makes you cough and choke.

The Varna lie scattered and stunned all around you, and the Doctor rushes forward to help Teron to his feet as a huge, booming voice echoes out of the mists.

'Bo Ho Ko Lo!' The language is strange and unfamiliar, but it's clear from the look of horror on the Doctor's face that he recognises it.

Crunching through the wreckage, a huge steel landing craft splits the town in two and a squad of armour-clad creatures stomp onto the jetty, immediately setting to work cuffing the Varna and bundling them aggressively into the rear of their transport.

The Doctor runs over, grabbing a small crimson cylinder from the leader's belt and speaking hurriedly into it.

'Language assimilated,' the creature responds, removing its helmet to reveal an unpleasant rhino-like head. As his men continue to clear the area of the alien monsters, the captain addresses what remains of the frightened colonists. 'We are the Judoon. Apologies for the inconvenience; these criminals will be removed from Betul and tried forthwith.'

He strides past you, stepping over your prone body to snatch Krane from Sean's grasp. 'We will take it from here, human,' he says.

'Er, good,' replies Sean, slightly confused.

'Thank heavens they turned up when they did,' says Rory, dabbing soot from Amy's cheeks with the sleeve of his shirt. 'I thought we were goners.'

'We all did,' says Mr Azzopardi, 'but we couldn't have done it without you. If you hadn't helped us out back there, the Judoon would have arrived to find us all dead.' He moves to shake the Doctor's hand, but is brushed aside by the furious Time Lord.

'There should have been another way,' he growls.

Go to 59.

The ghost town lies barren and empty as you wave off the Judoon landing craft and its cargo of refugees. Through the tearing mists you can just about make out the huge pillars of the ships, dark shadows in a sea of grey and, a few minutes later, the heat of their launch transforms the fog into a warm drizzle.

'All's well that ends well and all that,' says Rory, wiping his damp fringe from his forehead. 'A good day's work, I reckon.'

The Doctor doesn't respond and you ask him what's wrong. 'It's just a shame that they had to leave. If things had happened a little differently, who knows, maybe the humans and Varna could have learnt to share?' He brushes the thought from his mind and stamps his feet impatiently. 'Oh well, I guess we'll never know.'

'Can we get back to the colony now?' Amy asks the Doctor, 'I'm going to catch a cold if we stay out here much longer.'

You nod in agreement.

'Yeah, sorry, I'm being silly. A celebration is in order! Everyone is safe and sound; who could ask for more?'

'By "celebration", I assume you mean another round of tea?' Rory asks with a raised eyebrow.

'Is there any other way to celebrate?' The Doctor winks at you. 'Come on, let's get out of this rain.'

THE END

'Two hundred credits! Each!' Mrs Azzopardi can't believe her eyes as she flicks through the wad of notes the Judoon had stuffed into the colonists' hands before returning to their ships with the prisoners. 'I could build a second tea house with this!'

All around you the humans are laughing and cheering, their fear forgotten as they count their compensation. Even Amy and Rory are caught up in the celebrations, hugging each other with relief.

But one person isn't celebrating.

The Doctor stands at the edge of the jetty, peering into the hazy sky as the outline of the Judoon ships ascend through the clouds. You touch him on the shoulder and ask if he's all right.

'Do you know what the Judoon do to their prisoners?' he asks, and you shake your head. 'No, you wouldn't want to.'

He looks around him in disgust. 'Humans: so quick to forget things like that, especially if there's money involved.'

A feeling of guilt washes over you and you look down at the floor, eyes focused on the gentle movement of the water between the planks of the walkway. You mumble a quiet apology.

'It's not me you should be apologising to, it's the Varna. You had the chance to make things right and instead you just made them worse.' He turns and begins to walk across the harbour, back towards the TARDIS. 'Come on,' he says. 'I think it's time to take you home.'

THE END

'Hmmm, you're right; when you put it like that, breaking and entering the prison ships of the space police does sound like a pretty stupid idea.' The Doctor rubs his chin before deciding. 'Right, well, we can't just float around here looking like lemons all day then, can we? Let's say hi!'

Flashing you a cheeky grin, he gets to his feet, staggering slightly as the tiny boat pitches in the water with his movements. You hold on to the rudder for support, steering towards the closest ship as the Doctor windmills his arms, shouting, 'Hey, Judoon, over here! It's me, the Doctor!'

There are a series of dull thuds and suddenly you find yourself blinded as an intense white light floods onto the fishing boat from four huge spotlights mounted on the sides of the Judoon ships.

Over a loudspeaker, a deep, gruff voice intones, 'Language assimilated. Prepare to be boarded.'

'Boarded?!' the Doctor replies incredulously, shielding his eyes with his sleeve. 'Have you seen the size of this thing?'

Go to 62.

You tell the Doctor that it might be best not to draw attention to yourselves before you find out what's going on.

'You're right,' the Doctor agrees with a grin. 'Let's sneak on board.'

You draw the small rowing boat closer to the towering vessels as silently as possible, flinching as the oars splash loudly in the otherwise calm water. As you round the first ship, you spot a large hatch in the side, only a few feet above the surface.

'Good call.' The Doctor pulls on the rudder and the boat glides towards it.

Gingerly, the Doctor perches himself on the side of the boat and leans forward to inspect the solid iron hatch. 'Hmmm, looks pretty simple. The sonic screwdriver should get us in easily.' He fumbles in his jacket pocket before pulling out a long silver tube with an emerald crystal at one end, which he shines at the bolted lock.

A faint whirring sound fills the air and you watch, amazed, as the bolt slides back of its own accord. 'Sorted.' The Doctor winks at you as he slaps the device off and tucks it away once more.

With a squeal of unoiled hinges the Doctor pulls open the entrance to the Judoon ship and hauls himself over the ledge. 'Throw me the mooring line.' He gestures from the doorway. You find the coiled piece of rope and hand it up before taking his hand and climbing inside yourself.

'Hmmm, right. Well, it's a big ship and as long as we haven't set off any alarms, it should take a while for anyone to realise we're here.' The Doctor looks around, leaving you to tie the boat to the bolt on the hatch. Once satisfied that your getaway craft is secure, you follow the Doctor down the cold grey corridor leading towards the centre of the ship.

'First rule of sneaking:' the Doctor whispers, laying a hand on an interior door, 'assume things are safe until you discover otherwise.' With a jerk, the door swings forward and you stumble into a large, brightly lit room filled with nearly a dozen Judoon!

Twenty pairs of large eyes turn on you in an instant and beside you the Doctor slowly raises his hands. 'Actually, I think it was never assume,' he says quietly.

If you have access to a computer, click on box D on screen and enter the code word PRISONER.

If you do not, go to 38.

A few moments later you find yourself standing in the middle of Judoon Control. The top floor of their ship consists of a huge open space with curved consoles nested in concentric circles around the central command chair – where the Judoon captain is considering the pair of you. Outside the huge glass windows you can see the top of the fog curling just beneath the frame. Above the mists the rosy glow of the Betul sky bathes the room in a softness you suspect is rarely seen on the bridge of a Judoon ship.

You turn back to the Doctor as he flashes a small leather wallet at the Judoon captain, who stares at it with such intensity that you suspect his large horn might spear through it at any moment. After a brief pause the captain grunts and hands the paper back.

'There, see? The Doctor. Thought I might come along and assist you in your enquiries.' He nods in your direction. 'Me and my young friend are simply bursting to know why you've decided to come to this quiet little backwater planet so we can, er, help of course,' he says, tugging at his collar. 'Have the colonists done anything wrong?'

'The colonists have done nothing wrong,' the captain replies. 'They are in danger and we are here to help them.'

'In danger?'

'The Varna, an insectoid race of refugees, have decided that they, too, want to settle on Betul. But their proximity to the human colonies is against intergalactic planning regulations. We are here to punish them.'

'Punish them?' the Doctor swallows. 'That's a bit drastic, isn't it? Surely it's just a case of asking them nicely to move along?'

'No, they are aware of their violation of the law and in an attempt to avoid eviction they have resorted to acts of violence; attacking the nearby colonies and forcing them to retreat past the accepted legal radius so as to legitimise their settlement. These acts of aggression demand the strictest sentence. We must make an example of them and do so immediately before they strike again.'

The captain rises from his chair. 'Judoon platoon,' he barks to the nearby officers, 'form up! We are leaving.'

The Doctor turns to you. 'You know what? I think we'll tag along as well.'

If you think the Varna need to be moved on immediately before they cause any more trouble, go to 63.

If you feel you need to know more about these creatures before coming to any hasty decisions, go to 69.

There's no time to lose as you board the Judoon landing craft. The Doctor is behind you, ducking under the low ceiling and sliding into the seat next to you. He rubs a porthole with his sleeve and a faint stream of light illuminates the gloomy interior as the rest of the squad file in.

'It's a shame,' he muses. 'Why would anyone want to attack such a lovely little tea shop?'

'Maybe they don't like tea?' The Judoon captain growls, shifting into the other empty seat next to you, so that you find yourself flattened against the side of the craft by his huge bulk.

'Don't like tea?!' The Doctor looks incredulous. 'Blimey!'

With a huge crash, the landing craft is ejected from the side of the ship, hitting the water outside with such force that you would almost certainly have been thrown from your seat had you not been wedged in so tightly.

Through the porthole behind your head you can see the spray of the ocean as it races past you, tearing through the mist at incredible speed.

'Won't be long now,' the captain announces. 'Men: ready your weapons!'

A ripple of noise spreads through the craft as the squad check their equipment belts and arm their pistols, before grunting a series of swift affirmatives.

The Doctor nudges you gently and you turn to see him nod towards the window once more. 'Take a look at that beast,' he whispers.

Through misty glass you can see a huge, warped shadow approaching through the fog, and as it gets closer you realise that you're looking at a town! It appears to be floating on a wide raft, with tiny houses and dwellings stuck closely together in a weird sprawling mess. A small lookout post sits at the top of the structure and from it a mast supporting two large black sails on either side. A shiver runs down your spine as you spot a group of grotesquely humanoid shapes clambering and crawling across its surface. The Varna.

'We've arrived,' says the Doctor.

The captain rises to his feet. 'Maintain safe distance,' he calls to the pilot, 'and prepare the incinerator.'

'The inciner-what-or?!' The Doctor looks horrified. 'You mean to say you're going to fire at the settlement?'

The Judoon snorts stinking breath through its nostrils and eyes the Doctor. 'The law does not allow violent criminals to live,' he says simply.

'But you've not even met them yet! I thought you were meant to be police, not thugs!'

'They have attacked innocent civilians. I do not want to risk my men at the hands of these monsters,' the captain growls.

'But you're about to attack a defenceless settlement! How are you any less the monster?' The Doctor's voice lowers. 'This isn't justice – this is murder.'

He moves to get up and grab the pilot's arm before he can fire, but the Judoon captain pins him to his chair.

'Quick! Stop them!' he shouts. You throw yourself forward into the pilot's cabin.

If you have access to a computer, click on box F on screen and enter the code word INCINERATOR.

If you do not, toss a coin to see if your efforts succeed. Heads, go to page 64. Tails, go to 65.

It's too late and the portholes glow a deep crimson as the landing craft cannon sends a fireball hurtling towards the Varna settlement. There is a dull thud, and for a second you worry that it might not have worked.

Then comes the blast.

The shockwave makes the landing craft lurch wildly as the timber frame of the floating town disintegrates in a ball of flame. You look up at the roof of the craft as splinters of wood and debris rain down across the metal exterior, then out of the porthole to see the smoking wreckage of the town sink beneath the waves with a hiss of deep, black smoke.

Then you look at the Doctor.

His eyes seem suddenly sunken and tired; a worn old man in a young body. He shakes his head.

'It is done,' the Judoon captain growls. 'We will transport you to the shore so that you may leave. Your assistance was appreciated.'

The journey back to the TARDIS seems strange and dreamlike as you step onto the jetty at the edge of the human colony. Amy and Rory are waiting at the end of the walkway, bombarding the Doctor with questions about what they had seen from the café. But the Doctor doesn't respond and instead strides purposefully past them towards his ship, throwing open the doors and bundling you inside.

A moment later and you're standing in your garden once again, dazed and confused and alone, with the Doctor's parting words still ringing in your ears.

'You could have been a hero.'

THE END

'Ammo exhausted,' the pilot growls as you step back from the fire controls, sweat pouring down your face from the effort of stopping the Judoon. You turn slowly back to your seat, expecting to be rushed at any moment by the angry squad around you, but the captain's order is interrupted by the Doctor.

'Maybe now you'll be forced to face your enemies rather than hiding behind the barrel of a gun.'

'We aren't cowards.' The Judoon captain's eyes narrow.

'Of course you aren't,' the Doctor soothes him, flashing you a relieved smile. 'Which is why a tough man like yourself will take the moral high ground and give these creatures a chance to explain themselves before throwing them in jail.'

After a long pause the captain nods and gestures to his men. 'Prepare to board the settlement!' The Judoon salute in unison and stomp their feet as the craft swings around towards the front of the village.

With a gasping hiss of hydraulics, the front hatch descends onto the decking of the Varna settlement and the squad exits the craft, adopting a standard arrest formation, their guns at the ready. You step out into the cool, damp air behind them and suddenly you can hear the steadily rising chatter of the Varna as they realise the nature of their visitors.

You snap your head around, searching for signs of life until gradually, from out of the shadows, hideous insectoid shapes begin to form, loping into view to confront the Judoon.

An older Varna, with a mottled shell and pincers cracked with years of use, steps forward and hisses, 'I am Teron, leader of the Varna.'

'Quiet!' the captain barks. 'You are all under arrest. Anything you say can, and will, be used against you in a court of law.'

'We have done nothing wrong,' protests Teron, 'and if you persist in your arrest I promise you that we will not go quietly.'

'Invading the colonies of innocent humans is not "nothing",' the Judoon replies. 'You will suffer for your patent disregard for the law.'

'I'm not sure that's what he was trying to say,' the Doctor interjects.

If you want to let Teron have his say, go to 67.

If you can't take any more of his empty threats, go to 66.

You are outraged that these monsters could have so little respect for the human lives they have threatened with their irresponsible and illegal behaviour, whatever the Doctor says. You tell the Judoon captain to take them away before they offend your sensibilities further and the Judoon happily oblige, stomping forward to grab each creature by their bony wrists and slapping large steel handcuffs on them.

The Varna hiss and spit at their captors, their claws snapping out across the Judoon's armoured chests in defence, but the moulded rubber composite is too tough to be penetrated and their struggles only increase the brutality with which they are captured.

You step aside to join the Doctor on the decking as the Judoon bundle the distressed creatures into the landing craft. The captain turns to you as the hatch begins to descend.

'Are you coming?' he growls.

You look to the Doctor and he shakes his head slightly.

The Judoon shrugs and steps inside. With a clunk, the hatch closes and the landing craft begins to retreat out to sea. Behind you, you can hear the Doctor's boots against the wooden decking as he makes his way through the closely packed buildings of the Varna settlement.

You catch up with him as he begins to mount a narrow, winding staircase that leads to the lookout post at the highest point of the structure and ask him what the matter is.

'It wasn't fair,' he responds. 'You didn't give them a chance.'

You remind him of the acts that the Varna committed.

'A desperate situation can drive a race to do desperate things. Because of your swift judgement, the Judoon never gave them the chance to explain.'

At the top of the steps the Doctor leans out to grab the ropes hanging either side of the lookout posts and yanks them free to release the huge, tattered sails of the craft.

You watch as the wind tugs and pulls on the rough fabric until they fill and tighten and slowly, very slowly, the craft begins to glide towards the shore.

'Time to take you home, I think,' says the Doctor, his voice tinged with disappointment.

THE END

You agree with the Doctor: these creatures should be allowed to speak. How can the law administer justice without hearing both sides of the case?

Disappointed, the Judoon captain steps backwards and nods towards the creature.

'Thank you, human.' Teron's pincers snap and hiss gently at you as he swings his domed head this way and that. 'As I said, we had no choice. Our home planet was destroyed when the star it orbited went supernova and we had not yet advanced enough to build a space craft that could travel more than a few light years. It was only by chance that we found Betul in time. We have neither the resources nor the technology to leave this world and when the Judoon informed us that we were too close to the human colonies to remain on Betul, we had no other option. We know how the Judoon treat their criminals and we would rather die than be exiled to the Grobar Penal Colony.'

'The Grobar Penal Colony?' The Doctor looks aghast. He turns on the Judoon. 'You wanted to imprison them in the Grobar Penal Colony?'

'They are criminals. They deserve nothing less,' the Judoon captain retorts, avoiding the Doctor's eyes.

'But we have not killed anyone,' Teron counters, 'merely scared them. Humans find our race so unpleasant to look upon that they flee at the first sight of us.'

'It seems to me, Captain,' says the Doctor, almost shaking with rage, 'that it was you, the Judoon, who are to blame for this situation. Your insistence on following the law to the last letter has forced the Varna to commit the criminal acts that you are so eager to punish.'

The captain shifts uncomfortably before opening his mouth to speak.

'Don't you dare!' the Doctor hisses. 'Have you never heard of the "spirit of the law"? You jumped-up gang of pencil-pushers, you make me sick.'

A tense silence falls across the settlement before the Doctor finally composes himself and claps his hands. All eyes follow him as he strides into the centre of the deck.

'Right,' he says, looking around, 'I think it's time for a change of plan!'

Go to 68.

'We will not allow them to stay on Betul,' the Judoon captain growls. 'They are too dangerous to the human colonies.'

'Only because you won't let them stay.' The Doctor is swiftly losing his patience.

'Judoon do not take risks, it is unprofessional.'

By now the Varna have fully emerged from their houses on the settlement and have gathered on the deck, eager to see the outcome of the Doctor's frantic negotiation, well aware that their fates hang in the balance.

'But we cannot leave,' Teron reminds the Doctor, flexing his claws with frustration. 'It is impossible, we have no ship.'

The Doctor runs a hand through his floppy hair, sighing with exasperation. 'I know that, but they do!' He points his finger squarely at the Judoon. 'They're refugees; the law allows you to transport them to a new homeworld in times of need.'

'But no new homeworld has been designated; locating a suitable planet can take up to three hundred galactic working days before —'

'Yes, yes I know all that, but you're forgetting something. Me.' He flashes you a reassuring grin. 'I've been about a bit you see, and I know this section of the universe like the back of my hand.' He spreads his fingers by way of example and looks down. 'Ooh, that's new.' He rubs a scratch near his knuckle. 'In fact, I know a perfectly suitable little moon just north of the Prydone Nebula, barely a handful of light years from here. It's wet, tropical and, most importantly, uninhabited.'

Teron looks around at his comrades, grey eyelids blinking slowly across his huge inky pupils. 'Does that sound good?'

A huge hissing and gnashing of pincers erupts from the crowd and the Judoon squad step back, hands moving to their weapons before realising that the creatures are cheering!

What passes for a grin spreads across Teron's mottled jaw and he offers his hand to the Doctor. 'I think that's a "yes". Thank you, Doctor.'

'Well, I couldn't have done it without my friend here.' He reaches down to ruffle your hair. 'Quite the peacekeeper, this one.'

Solemnly Teron extends his claw, and you take it in your hand; the speckled joints are smooth to the touch and you shake it firmly. 'Thank you,' he says once more.

The Doctor tightens his bow tie and brushes down his sleeves. 'Right, top stuff! And if that's all, I think we'd better be off and leave you to it, gentlemen.' He raises a hand in farewell, then points at the Judoon captain. 'You,' he says. 'Behave.'

The captain nods.

The Doctor places a hand on your shoulder and together you turn and look out through the thinning mist at the shadow of the shoreline where Amy and Rory are no doubt still sitting in the café, oblivious to the events of the past hour. You smile to yourself: a job well done.

THE END.

You raise your concerns with the Doctor as you run along the steel corridor that leads down to the landing craft bay, trying to keep up with his ridiculously long strides. Isn't it a bit hasty to be running straight into a confrontation at this stage before you know the bigger picture? Surely time should be spent gathering evidence and building up a clear picture of the crime before rushing in to arrest the supposed criminals? They're refugees, after all.

The Doctor halts mid-stride and you almost run past him. 'You're right!' he declares. 'We're going about this all wrong: treating them as guilty until proven innocent, when it should be the other way around. These Varna have been through a hard time – who knows what's driving them to act against the surrounding colonies? Just because the humans were here first, doesn't make them innocent.'

He points to you and then taps his nose. 'There's more to this than meets the eye and together we're going to get to the bottom of it!'

If you have access to a computer, click on box E on screen and enter the code word STRATEGY.

If you do not, go to 8.

'There's no point arresting the Varna until we've fully investigated the crimes they've supposedly committed,' the Doctor argues with the Judoon captain sitting across from you in the cramped confines of the landing craft. The vessel rocks and shudders as it tears through the waves and the porthole behind you is blurred with mist. 'Let's go to the human colony and find out how they feel about the situation.'

The Judoon huffs through his large nostrils. 'Takes too long,' he growls.

'If justice is served then it shouldn't matter how long it takes,' the Doctor responds grimly. 'It is your duty to perform a thorough investigation.'

Without waiting for the captain's reply he turns to the front of the craft and shouts to the pilot. 'Take us to the colony, please, and step on it!'

The pilot shifts in his chair, uneasy about taking orders from anyone other than his superior. The captain snorts, but doesn't protest, and with a motion that slams your body against the cold steel wall of the vessel, the pilot swings the landing craft around in the direction of the shoreline.

The domes of the colony materialise out of the fog and soon the craft is crunching onto the pier of the harbour you'd left only an hour before. The front hatch hisses open and you join the Judoon as they step out onto the jetty.

'Can we keep the stomping to a minimum, please?' the Doctor asks. 'We don't want to scare the humans with yet another alien menace tramping mud all over their porches.'

You motion to the Judoon to keep the noise down, a finger pressed against your lips, before turning back in the direction of the colony.

Then your eyes widen in surprise.

'Actually, forget that,' the Doctor mutters. 'It looks like we're expected.'

From between the houses at the edge of the colony, a procession of villagers are picking their way across the harbour and, running ahead, you recognise Amy and Rory.

'Where've you been?' Rory calls out. 'You've missed all the excitement!'

At the head of the crowd, walking slowly between Mr and Mrs Azzopardi, is a Varna.

Toss a coin to see if the Varna is a prisoner or a free alien. Heads, go to 73. Tails, go to 72.

Better to go to the Varna settlement first – if you don't get there soon, they might do something they'll regret.

'Exactly, they're already in enough trouble with the Judoon,' agrees the Doctor.

A few minutes later you find yourself squashed between the Doctor and a Judoon in the darkened confines of the landing craft as it launches from the side of the ship, skimming across the waves in the direction of the Varna settlement.

As the spray arcs across the porthole behind you, you glance at the captain sitting next to you, then at the Doctor. He winks reassuringly. 'Don't worry about them. They've got good intentions – just a bit ham-fisted in their methods, that's all.'

At the front of the craft the pilot swivels awkwardly in his chair. 'Varna settlement coming into view, Captain,' he calls over his shoulder.

'Ooh, this should be fascinating.' The Doctor nods to the porthole behind you.

You turn and through the mists you can make out the jumbled silhouette of a large, ramshackle town. It appears to be mounted on a huge wooden deck, floating on a raft of barrels and steered by a pair of tattered black sails, several metres wide. The buildings themselves appear to have been built haphazardly, one on top of the other in an almost pyramid-shaped structure and as you approach, you realise that every window frame hosts a pair of large, black eyes.

The landing craft docks against the side of the settlement and a fresh breeze chills your face as the hatch descends. You step out blinking onto the deck, the Doctor close behind, then stop short as a loud chattering fills the air.

'Don't worry, they're just alerting each other to the fact we've arrived. Watch yourself though; humans don't tend to find their features very... pleasant.'

A moment later the whole town is crawling with Varna: long-limbed, inky-shelled creatures with talons on their hands and a row of bristling pincers in place of a mouth. They scuttle over every surface of the settlement with a seeming disregard for gravity as they make their way to the central area of the decking.

The Varna leader steps out of the shadows, his shell patched and mottled with age. 'What do you want, Judoon?' he asks.

'They're here to listen,' the Doctor replies.

Go to 74.

As the crowd approach, you realise that the monster is bound with rope and the citizens are acting as an escort for their prisoner.

'Er, are you the Judoon?' Mr Azzopardi calls out as he gets within earshot.

'We are,' the captain growls, marching forward to inspect the captive.

The Varna is tall and skinny; beetle-shell plates its body and huge black eyes border a mouth of pincers.

'We captured this little beasty when he and his mates decided to ransack our colony,' the tea shop owner explains. 'The Doctor's friends here said that you were some kind of space-police. Can you help us?'

If a Judoon could look smug, then the captain would have sneered at him as he spoke. 'They are wanted criminals; we will take care of them. Your colony is safe once more.' He turns to the Doctor. 'And you were wrong.'

The Doctor scowls and looks away, jogging over to Amy and Rory.

'I'm sorry, Doctor. I couldn't stop them; they were pretty angry about what happened,' Amy says.

'Too right,' says Rory. 'Those things did a proper number on this place. It's lucky everyone escaped with their lives.'

The Doctor looks over to the Varna as it surrenders to the Judoon.

'Did they hurt it?' he asks.

Amy looks away. 'I did my best.'

There is a loud click as a large pair of handcuffs locks over the creature's wrists before it is bundled into the back of the waiting landing craft. The Judoon captain salutes the crowd before turning to leave. 'Do not worry. We will deal with the settlement; apologies for the inconvenience.'

'Good riddance,' Mr Azzopardi snaps, turning to his wife. 'Come on dear, let's see what we can salvage from the shop.' She links arms with him as they make their way through the slowly dispersing crowd of colonists.

'Poor Mrs Azzopardi,' mutters Rory. 'She's had the life frightened out of her today. Still, nothing to worry about now, is there, Doctor?'

'Not for them,' the Doctor replies, gazing at the closing hatch of the landing craft.

'What do you mean?' asks Amy.

'The Judoon Captain,' he whispers. 'He said, 'deal'.'

Go to 35.

Amy runs towards you, ahead of the crowd, with Rory panting after her.

'Oh, thank God you're safe!' she gasps and gives you a hug.

'What happened here?' the Doctor asks.

'The Varna attacked us.' Rory bends over to catch his breath. 'But then we found one of them in the wreckage, Krane — he explained everything.'

'They weren't trying to hurt anyone. Just scaring people away so that they could stay — it's illegal to settle too close to a human colony without permission,' says Amy.

'And with faces like theirs, it's pretty tough to stop people running away long enough to make friends.' Rory adds, nodding over to Krane.

The Varna attempts to mask his bristling mouth with a long claw before realising that such a motion makes him look even more sinister. His large eyes widen with frustration, and his pincers clack nervously until the old woman next to him places a calming hand on his shoulder.

The Doctor smiles. 'Well done, the pair of you! You've done me proud today.' He turns to the Judoon captain. 'See?'

The Judoon opens his mouth to reply, but one of his squad-mates draws his attention, pointing to something out at sea.

The Varna settlement is returning through the mists, a jumble of misshapen houses flanked by huge black sails, all mounted on a large, floating raft.

A couple run up to you, with Krane striding forward between them.

'Why, it's Mr and Mrs Azzopardi from the tea shop! How are you?' the Doctor beams enthusiastically.

'We're okay, thank you, Doctor. Well, a little shaken,' Mr Azzopardi begins. 'But we're ready to talk to the Varna. Krane has explained everything – can you help us sort this out?'

'I'll try,' he replies.

With a thud the floating settlement arrives, and a great hissing erupts from its occupants as they realise that the Judoon are waiting for them.

'Teron! It's okay, come forward,' Krane calls over to his comrade. A mottled, greying Varna hops forward onto the jetty, eyeing the Judoon nervously.

'I am the leader of the Varna,' Teron begins in a hoarse, rattling voice. 'If you have anything to say, Judoon, you should say it to me.'

'Well actually, I have something to say, to all of you,' the Doctor interjects with a cheeky grin. He looks around and spreads his arms like a circus ringmaster. 'Gather round!'

Go to 43.

The Varna leader's legs fold themselves into a sitting position.

'We know it is illegal for us to build a settlement in such close proximity to another race's colony without mutual permission, but we had no choice. Our planet died and we hadn't the technology to travel further than a few light years. This was the only habitable planet within range; we cannot leave. Believe me, we would if we could.' He pauses and bows his head. 'When the Judoon gave us an ultimatum that we couldn't fulfil, we were forced to take drastic measures, attempting to scare the humans away, to create enough distance between us that the proximity laws did not apply. But we were too late.'

'You thought that breaking the law even further would save you from the Judoon?' asks the Doctor.

'And you think the humans would have reacted to us any other way? To them we are monsters,' the Varna retorts, holding up a long claw. 'But we don't act like monsters — we have never killed a human.'

'No, you're not monsters; you're scared and alone and right now you need someone to help you, not punish you.' A familiar fire sparks in the Doctor's eyes. He turns to you and smiles. 'So, it's a good job you've got us, then.'

You step forward, eager to offer your assistance, but the Judoon captain rests a hand on your shoulder. The Doctor holds up a finger.

'No, don't you dare try and stop us. Call yourselves policemen? You should be ashamed; you're bullies and nothing more.'

'Insulting a police officer is an offence.'

'Well, when you act like a police officer, I'll stop insulting you, how about that?' says the Doctor disgustedly.

The Judoon snorts. 'So, what do you suggest, Doctor?' he growls. 'They can't stay here.'

'They don't have to do anything,' says the Doctor, 'They can choose.'

If you think the Varna should return to the colony to try and make peace with the humans, go to 75.

If you think it's too late for peace between the races and that the Varna should move on, go to 68.

You tell the Doctor that you've all been through so much today, it would be a shame to just give up now. Where's the challenge in that?

'I like your gumption!' the Doctor grins. 'It's time to settle things with the humans. Just because you look different, doesn't mean you can't get on! Why, some of my best friends are ugly... no offence,' he adds quickly in response to Teron's hard stare.

He turns to address the crowd of hissing creatures. 'All right, Varna, it's time to stop feeling sorry for yourselves and start building bridges, maybe literally – it'll stop you needing to sail everywhere. So put on your best bow ties and let's go and meet the neighbours!'

A tentative cheer ripples through the nervous masses as the black sails billow in the wind and the settlement begins to float towards the shore, the Judoon landing craft bobbing along on a tether behind it.

The Doctor licks his hand and smoothes his hair off his face before nudging you. 'Come on, smarten up, we're about to make history!'

You pat down the wrinkles in your clothes, but before you can do anything more a shout goes up from the lookout post above. 'Land ho!' The human colony materialises out of the fog.

A moment later the Doctor's smile of anticipation is wiped from his face. Standing in the harbour, waiting for them, are the human colonists with Amy and Rory off to one side, looking shamefaced.

They have a Varna prisoner.

'Krane,' Teron murmurs quietly. 'We must have left him behind after our last assault.'

'They are merely defending themselves against your reign of terror, Varna.' The Judoon captain's voice drips with smugness. 'The law allows them to protect themselves and their families.'

'Oh, no.' The Doctor looks utterly heartbroken. 'Why do I get the feeling that this won't be going as smoothly as I'd hoped?'

If you think you can achieve peace between the races, go to 76.

If you think you can manage to save Krane, go to 77.

If you think all hope is lost, go to 78.

The settlement glides up to the jetty and you're the first to step off, making your way immediately towards Amy and Rory.

'You've missed the party!' Rory exclaims, relieved that you're safe. 'Although it looks like you've been having a bit of drama yourself.' He eyes the Judoon as they cautiously form a barrier between the humans and the Varna across the middle of the harbour.

But there's no time for pleasantries; the negotiations hang by a thread, and you need to stop the humans before they threaten anything they might regret. You run over to Mr Azzopardi, whose hand rests on the ropes binding Krane, and tell him to watch what he says: the Judoon only need the slightest hint that the humans won't tolerate the Varna to justify hauling them off to prison.

'Well, I reckon that's true.' Mr Azzopardi seems rather shocked at your empathy with the creatures that attacked his home. He looks over to the floating settlement behind you where the Doctor is talking furiously with Teron. 'How come you aren't dead?'

You explain everything: how the Varna are stuck here, how they never intended to harm any humans, how the law of the Judoon had driven them to acts of terror — and all the while Mr Azzopardi rubs his scruffy chin slowly, taking it all in.

'It makes sense,' Amy says suddenly behind you. 'The Doctor wouldn't bring them back here if he thought they were a danger.'

'Is this true, er, Krane?' Mr Azzopardi turns to his prisoner.

'Yes,' Krane answers simply.

You push the old man out of the way, in a hurry to untie the Varna before his comrades try and do so by force.

'What are you doing? That's our bargaining chip!' Sean the fisherman pushes through the crowd. 'If we give him back then we won't have any power to negotiate – they'll walk all over us.'

You point to the Judoon; they're on the humans' side and, knowing their no-nonsense approach, that's probably all they'll need. The Varna want to make peace, they don't need to be forced.

Mr Azzopardi turns to his wife. 'Do you think this is right, dear? I trust you.'

'Look at them.' Mrs Azzopardi points to you, Amy and Rory in turn. 'They don't live here, why would they wish us any harm? Of course I trust them!' She smiles. 'And the Doctor goes without saying; he's our best customer!'

You turn to see the Time Lord striding towards you, pleased to see Krane rubbing his arms, free at last. 'Are we ready?' he asks.

You nod.

Go to 43.

You hang back as the settlement thuds against the jetty. The colonists push their prisoner out ahead of them as they move forward to confront the Varna.

The Doctor turns to the Judoon captain.

'Don't arrest anybody until they've had the chance to talk. Let's keep the violence to a minimum before you start taking the Varna off-world.'

The Judoon captain nods. 'We will not intervene until violence between the races becomes inevitable.'

'Thank you,' the Doctor says before turning to address the crowd. 'Hello humans, let me introduce you to my good friend Teron and his people, the Varna! Now, I know you're angry, I know you've been hurt, but if you'll all just listen to me for a moment, I think I know how we can fix this.'

Mr Azzopardi steps forward.

'I know how we can fix this as well,' he calls over. 'You can have your comrade back if you promise to leave this planet and never return!' There is a chorus of agreement from the disgruntled colonists.

'Well, er, well...' The Doctor holds up his hand. 'Let me counter that proposal with, ah...' He pauses. 'Actually, that's basically what I was going to suggest; although maybe using slightly nicer phrasing.'

The Judoon captain turns to the Doctor. 'Really, Doctor? What do you have in mind?'

The Doctor lowers his voice. 'Okay, you win. They're never going to get on, and if people are going to start taking hostages then it's important to nip this feud in the bud. Right now my first priority is to get Krane safely back to his people – that's all I'm worried about.'

'And then?'

'You'll see,' the Doctor responds.

Go to 56.

Teron pushes past you, striding over to the edge of the deck as the settlement hits the jetty with a jarring thud. 'How dare they treat one of us with such little respect? We are not animals to be tied up and kicked around!'

The Judoon captain moves a hand to his weapon. 'Do not seek revenge.'

'Revenge? Revenge?! I am sick of those humans; they have taken our chance at a new life, destroyed our future and now they have tortured Krane! I don't want revenge, I want blood!'

'They can't have tortured him,' the Doctor says, looking across the harbour to where Amy and Rory are standing, their heads hung low. 'My companions wouldn't have allowed it.'

'Well, if the only people who would have protested are off-worlders like you, Doctor, then what does that say about the colonists?'

The Doctor has no reply, and Teron clicks his pincers triumphantly. 'I thought so.' He punches his claw in the air and emits a warbling battle-cry. 'Varna! We are at war!'

The creatures behind you echo the call and every Judoon on the deck moves for their weapons.

Go to 79.

Right now the only people who can stop this massacre are the Judoon. You pull the Doctor out of the way as the platoon draw their pistols, forming a partition between the angry Varna and the frightened colonists.

The creatures stop short as certain death is aimed at them down the barrel of a gun, and even Teron falters in his fury.

The Judoon captain finally declares what he has been desperate to say all this time. 'You are under arrest. Anything you say or do at this moment will be used against you in a court of law. Be warned.' He cocks his weapon.

'Listen to him, Teron,' the Doctor calls out. 'Better to live than die for nothing.'

'But it's Grobar!' Teron's eyes are filled with fear. 'I don't want to live out the rest of my days in that prison.'

'You've no choice, Teron,' the Doctor says sadly. 'The least you can do is go quietly; don't condemn yourself any further.'

Defeated, Teron drops to his knees, motioning to his comrades to follow suit. He holds out his wrists to the Judoon captain who slaps on a heavy pair of handcuffs, motioning to the trooper beside him to retrieve Krane from the humans and escort him into the back of the landing craft with the others.

'You had good intentions, Doctor,' Teron mutters as he is led away. 'But I think they may have been misplaced.'

'I wish you were right, Teron,' the Doctor replies quietly.

THE END.

You hardly dare to breathe as you crouch in the shadows, ears straining for sounds of the returning monsters. Suddenly, the Doctor touches your shoulder, motioning to you to keep your head down.

A quiet splashing reaches your ears, increasing in volume as the creatures leap elegantly from the banks of the shore to wade over to the front deck of the ghost town. The vessel tips slightly as they board and fear clutches at your heart as you listen to the clack of their claws on the wooden planks.

Agonisingly slowly, the Doctor edges along the side of the building to peer around the corner and you duck over to a small cluster of barrels nearby to try and find a better view.

The tall, thin, insect-like creatures mill about the village as they prepare to disembark, following the instructions of an older alien with a mottled shell; there are grey patches showing amongst the shiny black segments.

'Those claws look pretty lethal,' the Doctor whispers. 'I wouldn't want to get on the wrong side of that lot.' He scratches his chin. 'Have you noticed that, for a "ghost town" everything seems pretty physical?'

You remind him that he is stowing away on board their ship and 'physical' claws might not be something to emphasise at this precise moment.

'Good point,' the Doctor responds. 'I had wanted to stay hidden until we knew more about them, but that might make them angrier when they realise we've been here all along.'

Do you announce yourselves to the creatures? Go to 82.

Or do you stay hidden a while longer? Go to 81.

'We're here now, there's no point announcing ourselves 'til we've discovered more about these creatures,' the Doctor whispers. 'If nothing else, at least we'll have something to talk about when we are captured.'

What he says makes sense, but it doesn't stop you feeling any less scared as you edge closer to the monstrous group in front of you in an attempt to make out their conversation.

'Lip-reading is kind of useless on aliens with pincers for mouths.' The Doctor moves past you. 'We'll have to get within earshot.'

Dropping to the ground, you wriggle forward a few more metres, hugging the shadows until you're close enough that you can smell the stinking marsh-water that coats the creatures' bodies.

'Teron, our scare tactics aren't working – the humans will not move in time. We need to take more drastic action,' you hear one of the creatures say to its leader.

'The Varna are not a violent race. We will not resort to barbarism. Our aim is to survive, not start a war.'

'The Varna!' the Doctor exclaims. 'Never heard of them.'

You sigh and return your attention to Teron and his comrade.

'We've seen the Judoon ships; it's only a matter of time before they find us,' says the Varna leader. 'And if we have not secured our right to settle on Betul by legal means, then we will be arrested. The law will not forgive us if we harm the colonists.'

His comrade laughs. 'Arrest us? You think they will be so generous?'

'The Judoon are policemen — we will appeal to their better nature.' Teron's words are strong but his voice is shaking. In the shadows you can see a sadness fall across the Doctor's face.

'If they're relying on the Judoon's 'better nature',' he whispers, 'then they're in trouble.'

If it's time to reveal your presence, go to 83.

If you feel that there's still more to learn from staying hidden, go to 84.

'Best play it safe; we don't want to antagonise them.'

With a deep breath, the Doctor slowly steps out from the shadows, hands raised in the air. You follow suit.

'Uh, hello!' he grins cheerfully. Every neck on the vessel snaps towards you, huge black eyes wide with surprise and fear.

'Humans!' the leader hisses loudly, extending a talon.

'Well, that's not strictly true.' You realise that the Doctor is playing for time. 'My friend here is human, but me, I'm just an interested party...' he trails off, backing away towards the edge of the deck as the creatures surround you. Your shoes skid on the wet wood as you try to keep your balance.

'Your kind are in our way,' the leader continues, ignoring him. 'Leave your colony, or there will be consequences!'

'Well, that's not very friendly,' the Doctor replies with a frown. 'It's a nice colony.'

The leader sneers at you then, his mouth bristling with pincers. 'I'm glad you think so, because it's about to become your grave.' There is a whistle in the air and you jerk your head back just in time to avoid a fist of bristling talons.

'Jump!' The Doctor grabs your arm and pulls you into the water. The icy temperature shocks your lungs, but fear keeps you moving as you swim towards the shore. The Doctor gets there first, pulling himself up onto the bank and turning to search for signs of pursuit.

'It doesn't look like they're chasing us,' he says, wiping his face with a palm.

You grimace as thick black mud cakes your hands, turning slowly to see the ghost town lying silent and shrouded in shadow only a few metres away.

You haul yourself to your feet and the Doctor passes you a handkerchief that is far too small and delicate to make any difference to your sodden clothes.

'Okay, so that didn't go so well,' he says. 'At least Rory will be happy to see us, and by "happy", I mean smug.'

You make your way back into the colony slowly, and immediately bump into Amy and Rory standing just around the bend. Their arms are folded and they are sporting huge grins.

'Told you,' says Rory.

'Shut up,' says the Doctor.

Go to 17.

The Doctor turns to you. 'And I think that's our cue to enter and save the day!' He grins, stepping out of the shadows and striding straight over to Teron, his hand extended in greeting. 'Hello, Teron, pleased to meet you. I'm the Doctor and I've come to help!'

The Varna step back, chattering to each other, surprised at the strange man who has seemingly appeared out of nowhere. Teron looks down at the Doctor's hand, then back up at his face. 'Wait, what are you doing here?'

'Me and my friend were just quietly eavesdropping – it sounds like you've got yourselves in a bit of a pickle.' He calls to you over his shoulder. 'It's all right, you can come out now!'

Sheepishly, you rise from your hiding place and make your way over to the Doctor. The Varna close in around you, chattering suspiciously.

'So!' The Doctor rubs his hands together. 'Can we do anything to help?'

A slow smile spreads across Teron's pincers. 'I think you already have, Doctor. With hostages onboard, the humans will be forced to listen to us.'

The Doctor's grin vanishes. 'But we're not from the colony,' he explains. 'The people there couldn't care less what happens to us; they don't even know who we are.'

'He lies!' a Varna protests, but is swiftly hushed by Teron.

'Maybe, maybe not; either way, the Judoon will be unable to destroy our settlement with innocents on board.' He turns to you. 'Your hostage status is useful, so it's just a case of choosing which race to bargain with.'

Behind you the Varna grab your wrists, their sharp talons digging into your flesh.

'Any suggestions?' he finishes.

Would you rather be taken to the Judoon? Go to 86.

Or would you rather be taken to the colonists? Go to 90.

The Doctor pats his jacket pockets — he's getting bored — but you halt his fidgeting with a swift wave of your arm. From around the corner you can see another Varna, out of breath and heading in Teron's direction.

'Teron!' he pants. 'I've completed the census and we're one short!'

'One short?' the elder replies, eyes wide. 'How is that possible? Have we left one of our comrades behind?'

'It's Krane — he must have wandered off.'

'Or been captured. Who knows what the humans will do with one of our people?' spits Teron.

Suddenly there is a noise above your head and you look up to see one of the Varna crawling down from the lookout post at the top of the settlement; he hasn't seen you, but as his claws scrape against the sloped surface of the building above, he sends a shower of sawdust and splinters cascading down onto your head.

The dust fills your nose, making it itch and burn until, before you know it, you sneeze!

A deadly silence engulfs the settlement as Teron and his comrades turn in your direction.

The Doctor tugs at your sleeve. 'Looks like the game's up,' he says.

Slowly, you clamber to your feet and raise your hands in the air.

Do you offer to help the Varna? Go to 87.

Or do you demand that they leave the colony, and this planet, in peace? Go to 85.

You decide that the best course of action is to attempt to turn the tables on your captors before they try and slice you up. Stepping forward, you provide Teron with an ultimatum: stop terrorising the humans, whatever the reason, or you and the Doctor will stop them instead.

You swallow in the stunned silence that follows, turning to look at the Doctor in search of some kind of approval, but the Time Lord simply shakes his head.

'I don't think you should have done that,' he mutters. 'We weren't here to make threats, we were here to understand.'

With an angry clatter of pincers Teron raises a grey-tinted claw. 'See, Varna, how the human threatens violence against us? I fear for Krane's safety at the hands of these animals.'

He strides over to you and you set your jaw in defiance. 'Although now...' he muses, 'now, we have hostages of our own!'

'That won't do you any good,' the Doctor yelps as his hands are grabbed by a group of Varna and he is yanked roughly onto a nearby crate. 'The humans don't know us, we're from off-world, we mean nothing to them. If anything, you should take us to the Judoon — there I have some authority. I have worked with them in the past and I might be able to talk them into reconsidering your situation.'

'Our situation is getting better and better by the minute, Doctor,'

Teron spits. 'The Judoon wouldn't dare fire upon a settlement containing innocents.'

'But we can help you in so many other ways!' the Doctor pleads.

'Silence!' the Varna snaps. 'I need time to consider how best to use you and I cannot concentrate with all your incessant chattering.'

The Doctor falls silent, and a few minutes later Teron makes up his mind.

Does he choose to take you to the human colony? Go to 90.

Or the Judoon fleet? Go to 86.

'It won't matter what we say to the humans at this stage. The Judoon are literally on our doorstep – we must confront them.'

'Well, they're not literally on your doorstep,' the Doctor smirks.

'They will be,' Teron growls before turning to his comrades in the lookout post and bellowing, 'Varna, hoist the sails!'

Slowly the deck begins to move beneath you as the huge black sails of the ghost town swell in the breeze, and soon the settlement is ploughing through the water at surprising speed for such an unwieldy construction.

Cool spray peppers your face and you blink away the drizzle to see the huge, towering shapes of the Judoon ships, half-submerged beneath the water, and even the Doctor can't suppress a 'wow!' at the sight of them.

'Move!' The Varna behind you jabs you in the back with its claw, pushing you along the deck until you are standing right at the front of the craft. The Doctor joins you a minute later, almost skidding off the edge as his shoes lose their grip on the wet floor.

'You're expecting us to walk the plank in front of them?' the Doctor asks.

Teron laughs bitterly. 'No, it's merely a precaution; the Judoon have been known to incinerate illegal settlements from a distance, but with two innocent bystanders in full view, they'll think twice before turning the cannons on us before we've had our say.'

There is a dull thud as, from several stories above sea level, three floodlights arc down from the side of the Judoon ships, throwing the ghost town into sharp relief.

The Varna cover their eyes, dazzled by the bright light, and you grab the Doctor's hand in the confusion – this is your chance to escape!

If you dive for cover, go to 88.

If you think it's better to stay where you are, go to 89.

The Doctor takes advantage of the stunned silence. 'I'm sorry — really sorry — that we snuck on board your lovely, er, ghost town.' He screws up his face at the phrase. 'But we came to help, not to deal or threaten or fight.'

The Varna look to Teron. 'And why would you want to do that?' he asks.

'The humans in that colony are quiet, peaceful folk; they just want to get on with their lives, as I'm sure you do. I have no wish to see either side suffer, and if it's the Judoon that are driving you to invade the neighbouring settlements, then maybe I can do something about that. I've dealt with the Judoon before, I know how they work, and we can act as ambassadors for both races if you'll let us.'

Teron nods. 'The Judoon have ordered the impossible. Our homeworld is dead and our technology is limited. Only a few of us survived on the journey to this world and we have neither the skill nor the resources to leave.'

'Then why have they ordered you to leave?' the Doctor asks.

'Because we have settled in human territory without permission, and although we need not disturb the colonies with our settlement, the only way to legally remain on Betul is to create a large enough distance between us and our neighbours to declare this area of water our own.'

'And that's why you've been attacking the colonies, to try and persuade them to relocate?' asks the Doctor.

'Exactly.'

'I see.' The Doctor rubs his chin.

'We wish the humans no harm; our physical appearance is enough to drive them away,' says Teron.

'I can't imagine they'd be likely to invite you over for a cuppa, that's for sure,' the Doctor smiles.

Go to 93.

It's now or never and you pull the Doctor into the ocean with a huge splash. You flounder for a second, shocked at the deep, penetrating cold of the icy water, but soon you manage to steady yourself and begin swimming away towards the shoreline.

'Wait!' the Doctor splutters, treading water whilst trying to wipe his wet fringe from out of his eyes. He turns back to look at the ghost town, a monochrome image picked out in black shadows and white highlights. Slowly, the beams of light waver over the settlement and its occupants. Then, as suddenly as they had appeared, the lights are shut off, plunging the area into gloom once more.

'I don't like the look of this,' says the Doctor. 'Why haven't they launched any boarding craft?'

His fears are confirmed when the gruff voice of a Judoon echoes around the still water.

'Varna, your illegal settlement on this planet and the acts of violence you have committed on the neighbouring human colonies have incurred the maximum possible sentence. Prepare to be incinerated.'

'No!' the Doctor shouts, paddling desperately towards the Judoon ship as the occupants of the Varna village begin to abandon their craft, diving into the water to avoid the incoming blast. 'You can't do this! It's not right! They've killed no one – your information is wrong!'

But it's too late; a huge fireball arcs out from the summit of one of the ships, plummets directly into the Varna settlement and engulfs the town. The shockwave pushes you beneath the surface and you struggle for air, floundering in futile desperation.

A moment later you feel the firm hand of the Doctor grab your clothes and haul you to the surface. Through great whooping breaths you ask him what happened.

'It's over,' he replies grimly.

THE END

You tell the Doctor that you'd better stay here; it might not be the most useful job in the universe, but right now standing in plain sight of the Judoon might be the only thing stopping them from destroying the ghost town completely.

The Doctor nods. 'Not exactly my most heroic move to date, but you've got to work with what you're given.'

You squint through the glow and can just about make out a series of small orange rectangles opening along the hull of one of the Judoon ships.

'Launch bays,' the Doctor explains. 'They're sending a squad over.'

A second later you can see the small steel rectangle of a landing craft being fired into the ocean, bobbing to the surface before steering towards the ghost town. 'Prepare to be boarded.' The gruff voice of a Judoon echoes out of a loudspeaker mounted on the front of the vessel and the Varna push forward around you, eager to protect their hostages.

With a thud, the landing craft hits the deck, and the front end splits away with a hiss of hydraulics to reveal a squad of black-armoured Judoon. The wooden decking of the settlement creaks as they step out of their craft, the leader removing his domed helmet to reveal a huge, horned face. He places his hands on his hips and looks around accusingly.

'Varna, you are under arrest. Hand over the human hostages and come with us.'

Teron grabs you by the shoulders. 'We will not hand over the hostages until we have discussed terms!'

The Doctor groans. 'Don't try and bargain with a Judoon,' he says. 'That's just asking for trouble.'

'The Judoon have no need to discuss terms,' the captain barks. With surprising speed he strides over to you, batting the Varna away with his fist as if swatting a fly. Teron moves as if to retaliate, but the loud clack as the squad arm their pistols makes him think twice. He hangs his head in defeat, and a single tear slides across his mottled face.

'I see we have no choice,' he whispers sadly. 'Varna, surrender – I have failed you.'

The Judoon move forward and the sound of handcuffs being snapped into place spreads across the ghost town as the creatures are catalogued and bundled into the transport.

Teron is the last to duck into the shadow of the landing craft, and as the hatch hisses and begins to close he turns to you one final time. The sadness in his eyes makes you choke.

'I apologise,' he says. 'We would never have hurt you – either of you – but we had no choice.'

'I believe you,' says the Doctor, sadly.

The Judoon captain stomps up to you. 'You are free to go. If you require compensation for your troubles, or transport to the human colony—'

'No, that won't be necessary,' interrupts the Doctor. 'We can make our own way home.'

The Judoon nods and boards his craft. You stand on the deck, watching as it pulls away towards the towering ships, and the Doctor rests a hand on your shoulder.

'When I say home, I mean home.'

And it's then that you realise your adventures with the Doctor are over.

THE END

'We're holding humans hostage; we should take them to the other humans,' Teron decides out loud. 'The Judoon might give as little thought to their lives as they do to ours.'

The ghost town keels around and you set your shoulders, trying hard to hide your fear. The Varna tie your hands with surprising delicacy considering the sharpness of their claws and you are lined up on the front deck of the craft as it glides towards the domed outline of the human colony.

All around you the creatures hug the shadows, their dark shells swallowed by the blackness between the jagged angles of their rickety dwellings and you realise in an instant that they're scared!

'Scared of the Judoon, maybe,' the Doctor muses, 'but of the humans? I mean, I've met some scary humans in my time, but Mr and Mrs Azzopardi aren't scary. Are they scary? Maybe if you had a phobia of people who were too nice...' He turns in his bonds to look over to where Teron is busy barking instructions to the Varna in the lookout post high above. 'Teron! What is it about the colonists that makes you so scared of them? Wasn't it meant to be the other way around?'

Teron laughs, a staccato burst that hurts your ears. 'Doctor, we do not fear the humans, but with the eyes of the Judoon watching our every move we must be careful not to let them provoke us into doing something we will regret.'

The Doctor turns back to the shore. 'You and me both,' he mutters as the harbour slips into view, revealing the colonists crowded up against the shoreline, waiting for them.

Do they hold a Varna prisoner? Go to 91.

Or have they befriended their captive? Go to 92.

'Comrade Krane! The humans have taken him prisoner!' the Varna in the lookout post calls down from his perch and the Doctor groans as his worst fears are confirmed. You turn to remind him that Amy and Rory have been there to sort things out; it might not be so bad.

'You might be right.' The Doctor cocks his head. 'But you know I said humans weren't scary? Well, on their own they're not, but put a whole bunch of them together before trying to scare them from their homes and you've got an angry mob!'

And the mob certainly looks angry as it parades its prisoner onto the jetty. Amy rushes as close to the ghost town as she dares, almost in tears.

'I tried, Doctor, we both did, but they wouldn't listen.'

'Have they hurt Krane?' the Doctor calls over.

'No, they might threaten to, but they don't have it in them.'

Mr Azzopardi steps forward, interrupting the reunion with a sharp cough. 'Uh, hi.' He pauses, composing his thoughts. 'We've got one of your kind here, monsters, and we thought that you might want him back enough to stop invading our colony and talk.'

'Don't do anything stupid, Teron,' the Doctor whispers in the Varna's ear as he steps to the front of the craft. 'Agree to a fair exchange, and then maybe you can negotiate without hostilities.'

'A fair exchange?' The Doctor hadn't realised that Mr Azzopardi was in earshot. 'We barely even know that pair, they're not from here!'

'What?!' The Doctor is incredulous. 'I'm your best customer! That hits me where it hurts.'

But the old man merely folds his arms. 'If you want us to give your comrade back, then we have a few requests you need to follow before we do. We want you to leave our colony, and this planet, in peace!'

The Doctor winces. 'I wish you hadn't said that.'

'I'm sorry, human, but that is impossible,' Teron hisses angrily. 'The Varna cannot leave, and if you won't return comrade Krane to us then we will take him by force!'

The Varna erupt from the shadows, spilling out onto the jetty, hissing wildly and flashing their claws. The crowd steps back and in the confusion the Doctor unties your bonds.

'It's time to make a run for it, I think!' he says.

You ask him what happened to his ropes.

'Ropes? I'm a Time Lord! Do you really think I've lasted this many centuries to be defeated by ropes? I'm quite offended.'

And with that he grabs your hand, yanking you off the settlement and onto the rough wooden planks of the harbour walkway.

Go to 57.

'It's comrade Krane!' a Varna shouts from the lookout post.

The Doctor closes his eyes and holds his breath.

'He's free!'

'Oh, good,' the Doctor sighs, visibly relieved. 'I knew I could count on that pair.'

Teron steps over to stand in front of you, his eyes showing every year of his considerable age.

'Well, Doctor, it looks like I was wrong about the humans. You were right; maybe we should have given them the chance to hear us out.'

'Well they already might have, thanks to Krane's little accident of being left behind.'

With a swift snap of his claw, Teron slices the ropes that bind your hands and then moves to release the Doctor. The Time Lord holds his wrists up to his face to inspect them and, seemingly satisfied, proceeds to clasp the Varna's claw and shake it firmly.

'You don't know how glad I am to be right,' he says. 'Sometimes humans can surprise you.'

'Well, let's hope they continue to,' says Teron. 'It's not over yet.'

With a loud thud the Varna settlement reaches the shore.

Go to 94.

A few minutes later the Doctor is bounding around the deck, spurring the Varna into action with his infectious enthusiasm.

'Okay, well if I know the Judoon like I know the Judoon, then they'll be sticklers for paperwork. If they won't allow you to settle on Betul because you don't have planning permission, then we'll just have to go and get it before they arrive to take you away.'

'But... how?' Teron is confused.

The Doctor looks puzzled. 'The same way everybody gets planning permission – by asking the neighbours! Varna: set a course for the human colony. It's time to go and rescue Krane!'

In the lookout post above, the Varna haul the ropes guiding the sails, adjusting the angle to pull the ghost town around, and in no time at all you're heading back to the shore.

'That's all very well, Doctor,' says Teron, 'but the humans are hardly likely to consent considering how we've attacked their homes. Who knows what they might have done to our comrade in revenge?'

'Have faith, Teron,' the Doctor replies. 'The colonists are gentle folk and I think, above all, they'll be relieved to hear that the attacks are over. It's just a question of phrasing it right.'

You tug on the Doctor's sleeve and he turns to follow your gaze. The dark shape of the harbour is approaching through the fog and there, waiting for them on the jetty, is the entire population of the colony.

'Right,' says the Doctor, 'here we go!'

Toss a coin to see if Krane is a prisoner or a free man. Heads, go to 94. Tails, go to 95.

Amy and Rory rush to meet you as you step off the deck and onto the jetty.

'You're all right! Thank God!' Amy gathers you up in her arms.

Rory puts his hands on his hips. 'Well, we thought we were pretty good to make friends with Krane here, but now you've gone and got a whole town of them! Always got to go one better, haven't you, Doctor?'

The Doctor grins. 'I knew I could count on you. Is Krane okay?'

'He's fine,' calls a voice from the crowd.

'Mr Azzopardi! How nice to see you again, and Krane!' He waves to the mismatched pair as they step through the colonists and across to your group. 'I've heard all about you.'

'Then you will be pleased to know that the humans have heard of our plight and they sympathise.'

'I think 'sympathise' is a bit of an understatement,' says Mr Azzopardi. 'My poor wife was bawling her eyes out the moment Krane opened his mouth!'

Krane turns to his comrades as they disembark, cautiously edging towards the crowd of humans on the banks. 'It's all right brothers,' he says. 'We are welcome in their land.' The Varna chatter excitedly and push forward, each one eager to be the first to meet their new friends.

'I see you were right once again, Doctor,' says Teron. 'I am glad.'

'Me too!' says the Doctor, mopping his forehead with a handkerchief. 'I was worried for a minute, but I knew Amy and Rory wouldn't let me down. I choose my travelling companions too carefully for that.' He ruffles your hair affectionately.

'So, what happens now?' asks Teron. 'Should we stay here and wait for the Judoon together? I worry that if we confront them alone, then we may not be believed.'

Go to 42.

95

'Come on, Amy, Rory, do me proud.' The Doctor crosses his fingers as the people on the bank begin to take shape. 'Tell me that Krane is safe and sound.'

With a jolt the ghost town thuds against the harbour jetty, making you stumble onto the wooden walkway. The Doctor strides past you. He looks around keenly as the citizens of the colony stand open-mouthed at the sight of the Varna in front of them. Suddenly, he spots Amy and Rory off to the side. He half-waves in their direction and raises an eyebrow.

Amy shakes her head slowly.

'Oh no,' the Doctor whispers.

There is a cough from amongst the crowd and you are surprised to see Mr Azzopardi pushing through the onlookers. A frightened hush falls and the humans part to reveal a Varna, bound tightly with rope, following the tea shop owner out onto the jetty.

A great protest erupts from the Varna and Teron's wide eyes narrow. 'Doctor, what have your friends done to our comrade?'

'Nobody who ties up an innocent creature is my friend,' the Doctor replies grimly. He turns to Mr Azzopardi. 'What have you done? The Varna were here to make peace!'

'We don't want peace, Doctor,' the old man retorts. 'We want them to take their buddy here and leave.'

'But the Judoon will arrest them if you don't—'

Mr Azzopardi cuts him off. 'Not our problem. Those creatures have attacked our homes and scared my wife half to death; they are not welcome here.'

Hurriedly, he unties the prisoner, pushing him forward towards the ghost town with shaking hands.

'Look, there you go! He's free! No harm done. Just go.'

Teron moves forward, catching Krane in his claws and inspecting him for any signs of injury, but there are none. He looks to the Doctor.

'Maybe it is for the best,' he says. 'We have brought these humans more harm than good. I think we should let them alone now.'

If you agree with Teron, go to 96.

If you decide that you shouldn't give up and want to help them confront the Judoon, go to 97.

Amy rushes forward to help Krane onto the deck of the Varna settlement, touching his hand tenderly.

'I'm sorry,' she says. 'I wish things had turned out differently.'

Krane turns to her but says nothing. She steps back to join the Doctor, Rory and you on the jetty as the craft pulls away from the shore.

'Take care Teron!' The Doctor shouts after them, but their response is muffled by fog.

'Safe at last.' Mr Azzopardi heaves a sigh of relief, hugging his wife tightly to his chest. 'Looks like you managed to talk some sense into those creatures, Doctor.'

The Doctor looks grim. 'Yes, but now I realise that it might not have been the Varna that needed sense talked into them.'

Mr Azzopardi sniffs and turns away, following the crowd of citizens as they make their way back to the colony.

'We tried our best,' says Rory.

'And it wasn't good enough,' snaps the Doctor. 'Now those creatures are at the mercy of the Judoon with no one to vouch for them; no defence, no chance.'

Sulkily, the Doctor thrusts his hands into his pockets and stomps off towards the buildings, leaving you to pick your way across the muddy walkways behind him.

Go to 39.

You run after Teron as he helps Krane onto the deck. If the colonists won't aid them in their confrontation with the Judoon, you will.

The Doctor is at your side in an instant. 'That's the spirit, never give up!' he pants.

'And we're coming too; it's the least we can do to make up for what happened here.' Amy and Rory are standing at the edge of the jetty, eyes wide in amazement at the sight of the craft; its jumbled architecture strangely beautiful in the hazy afternoon light.

The Doctor frowns. 'So, what makes you suddenly so sympathetic to the Varna's plight?'

'Because you're sympathetic and we trust you,' Amy shrugs.

'That doesn't sound like a very good reason,' the Doctor sniffs.

'Then what's your reason?' Rory jumps to Amy's defence.

'My reason is that if something goes wrong, and I didn't do everything in my power to prevent the Varna from coming to harm, then I will never forgive myself.'

Rory nods. 'Yeah? Well, that's our reason, too.'

The Doctor throws his hands up in the air, trying to hide an affectionate smile, then holds out his arm to pull them on board.

The sails unfurl once more and the colonists remain standing, staring at you, dazed and confused by what just happened in the middle of the marshy harbour, until finally they are swallowed up by the fog.

'What happens now?' Amy asks the Doctor, stamping her feet to keep warm.

The Doctor checks his watch and turns to peer into the gloom all around you, searching for signs of life.

'We wait,' he says finally.

Go to 53.

'"Colonists have once again been driven from their homes along the Betul coastline by mysterious entities, who are attacking settlements under cover of the monsoons.

Eyewitnesses report seeing an unearthly ghost town materialise out of the mists, populated by strange, monstrous inhabitants."'

The Doctor pauses and squints at the grainy, unfocused photograph on the front page. You can just about make out the dark silhouette of a large floating object on the sea. The Doctor frowns and resumes his reading.

'"Accounts describe menacing insects covered in ichorous shells and dripping with ocean slime. It is rumoured that their screeching voices can drive humans insane and their claws could sever the head of a human with one blow... but no such casualties have been reported at this time."'

The Doctor snorts.

'Ha! Journalism: nothing changes. Why let facts get in the way of a good story?'

Amy silences him with a stern glance and the Doctor swiftly clears his throat.

'I'll just shut up and keep reading, shall I? Okay. "Our own Colony Seven is the last settlement left and our townspeople have vowed to remain resolute during tonight's forecast monsoon. They are building reinforcements and taking precautions to defend themselves against anything that might approach during the rains."'

Go to 10.

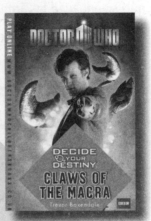